RAVAN'S WINTER

To my friend Tom!
Best Wishes!

9·6·14
Spokane

Advance Copy

Ravan's Winter

by

F.A. Loomis

DEDICATED TO

DONALD REXFORD

Storm Peak Press c/o Lulu.com
5203 West Silverlake Lane
Boise, ID 83703

© 2014, Floyd A. Loomis
ISBN 978-1-105-92303-6
Library of Congress Catalog Card Number: pending

South Fork Elk Fork

a truck on the road,
tufts of cattle hair in barbed wire,
crickets in pastures, sagebrush laden
with dusty green berries,
abandoned threshers, rickety corrals,
newborn calves with mitten ears,
a young deer yearns to walk,
nibbles brush, cheeks flutter,
black eyes and nose shine

bluebell streams in foothill draws
a white sun in streaks of cloud—
an egg in a scratchy nest—
weathered gray fences and shacks,
lush bottomland, evening coolness,
cobblestone trails, dusty log decks,
deadfall of yellowpine, lodgepole and fir,
grass smoke in willows,
a burn smell in sawdust and slabwood

old lanes mantled with dust,
springy pine cones, gnarled aspen,
barbed wire draped in yellow
snapdragons and white lilac
old graves hidden by pine needles, plastic
flowers for baby boy hardin, sara bell &
buck barker, nellie & rebecca canaga,
frank lacy mcfall, emma lee jasper,
orville kent apple, dollie mae ireland,
c.e. (ned) blackstone, dirk lucas

woodpeckers, chattering grosbeaks,
sunlight falls into the truck cab,
a maladjusted movie projector
in black pines a coyote picks its way
through the braided grass of a squirrel colony,
then wanders into darkness, dusty willows,
over broken, red marble bark,
into deeper thickets with no
afterglow of pink and pale yellow

GONE TO SEED

Frank was down from the mountains, his summer job managing a logging company's machine shed and Indian brush crew ended. The Navajos were back on the bus to New Mexico. He slid the first draft of the poem back into the manila envelope with some others.

At the gate a dog met him. A cross between bulldog and Australian shepherd, it tried to bite him as he walked between the gateposts. Frank knew the game, however, and had already picked up a stick. He threw it as hard as he could and the dog veered off toward hog pens beside the barn.

He stepped over a calf halter next to a bicycle and dented wagon and passed a horse chomping on the tendrils of a weeping willow next to the kitchen window. When the dog returned with the stick, it ran too close to the horse's hind legs and the horse kicked hard, sending it rolling and yelping into a raspberry patch. The horse kicked again, sending a plastic chainsaw case banging across the ground and into a syringa bush. Several clucking chickens charged out from under the white lilac followed by a second dog with sagging red gums and a puny nose. It growled at the horse, then found its way back to its dirt bed.

Frank eyed the inventory of additional obstacles, then stepped over a crumpled, rust-colored canvas irrigation dam and up the steps to the front porch of the house. Through a window he noticed a figure walking across the living room. The boy came to the door as Frank knocked. "Hello, Dillon," Frank said, looking at the Lucas boy with his black, ten-gallon cowboy hat pulled down so tightly over his head that his ears seemed to grow sideways.

"Hi Frank," said Dillon, who was so shy that every exchange of words was uncomfortable.

From the kitchen Bern saw Frank and ran to meet him. She gave him a kiss on the cheek and screamed, "Frankie, we've all missed you so much. We're so glad you're here." She put her arm around him and they walked into the kitchen to see SueLee, Bern's mother.

Out the window Frank noticed Vernon Lucas in the timber behind the house. He appeared to be putting fertilizer into a horse-drawn spreader. Somehow it was a comfort to be around the Lucas family, old family friends, though their household was always in chaos and tended to give Frank a headache if he stayed around too long. Their oldest son Dirk had been killed in Vietnam, blown up in his sleep by a mortar round. It had been nearly a year since the death. Most of the family was over the pain, but Vernon carried the burden of knowing he had encouraged Dirk to enlist. His son's death had taken away his sociable nature and whenever Dirk's name was mentioned he had a feeling as if sharp wire were pulling across the inside of his chest. He seemed often to think about how it would have been different had he not encouraged his son's interest in the military.

Frank had stopped by to say hello and to share news about his own plans to exit the military. He was currently a Navy ROTC candidate in the second year of college. His grandfather Percy was

getting old and had few opinions about the service, so Frank
gleaned all the advice he could from other family members and
neighbors.

Bernice had grown up with Frank and they had always been
close, often taking walks along the Timber Trail between the two
ranches, confiding innocently in one another about people in the
community and personal events in their lives. Frank had played the
role of big brother to Bern, especially after Dirk had joined the
army four years earlier.

SueLee looked the same in her long calico skirt and dirty apron
as Frank kissed her chubby cheek, then they all sat down in the
kitchen beneath a piece of embroidery hung above the stove. The
embroidery was edged crudely with little red roses and black
leaves. It said, "God Watches This Home." There was broken glass
under one kitchen chair and near the back door an earthen pot full
of blooming daisies. A huge black, yellow, and white thermometer
with PENNZOIL written on it hung outside the kitchen window.
The horse in the front yard had moved to the back of the house
now and was nibbling a bush by the weather thermometer.

Frank also noticed above the kitchen table a photograph of an
Arabian stallion and rider thumb-tacked to the wall, a curling
family portrait, and a Woolworth-framed print of some steep,

snowy mountains and a lake. On the bathroom door across the
room hung a green poster of a mountaineer with a rifle that said,
"A place to sleep, plenty to eat, a world of beauty. Kings never had
it better."

Bern looked admiringly at Frank. "I wasn't sure what college
would do to you, Frankie, but I still recognize you. It's the same
old Frankie."

"Well, what did you think would happen to me?"

"Well, I thought you'd be in a uniform by now, for one thing."

"I don't wear it all the time, Bern. Besides I have two more
years of hard labor before they let me fly."

Bern was too busy with farm duties to stay in her seat. She rose
and walked across the room to put a handful of leather strips into a
large tin tray. After putting them in the tray, she set it on an old
trunk next to the stove. The trunk was spitting out shirtsleeves,
long underwear legs, and what looked like part of a lavender
curtain. Frank couldn't take his eyes off Bern's long red hair that
touched her waist, and when she turned he admired her dark eyes
the color of elk hide that glistened under florescent kitchen lamps.
He did not care that there was a smudge of dirt around her mouth.
She had been at chores.

"Let me get you coffee, Frank," SueLee said, adding, "Bern, go tell your father Frank's here."

Bern dashed out the back door and yelled at Vernon.

"What's happened around here? Bern's already a woman, SueLee."

"Oh, don't remind me. She gets telephone calls now from young men; can you believe it? She's only fifteen. Fortunately, we're still on the party line, so Ayla Morrison or Laurie Rowe tell me if the boys sound fresh with her. I had to tell one of them to stop calling recently."

"I haven't been gone that long," Frank muttered to himself.

"What was that?" asked SueLee, her eyes studying Frank.

"Oh, nothing. I'm just talking to myself."

"Sit down there, Frank," she said. "Here's a jar of my best zucchini pickles and there are some chocolate cupcakes." She placed the pickles on the table. "The coffee will be a minute. I'll finish cubing this butter." She lifted a short wooden box that had hinges on one side and slammed it into the large yellow cake of butter she had just salted liberally. She ran her fingers across both ends, making them smooth, then opened the box and dropped a large cube of butter onto a sheet of waxed paper. She repeated the process. "Are you getting ready for Seattle?"

"I'll be here for a week before I leave."

"Still in the Navy ROTC program?"

"Oh, yes I am, but I've thought about getting out."

"I thought you were just getting started on your career."

Just then Grandma Thelma walked in from the root cellar carrying strings of dried apricots, prunes, and wax beans. Her hair was as white as a cloud as she sat down at the table, breathing heavily. "Land a'mighty! It's Frankie Ravan. How are you there, Frankie m'boy?"

"Hi, Thelma. You sound winded."

"What's that you say?"

"I say you sound tired."

"Oh. Those ten steps to the cellar are a mountain to me, but it's good to get the exercise. How's Percy since Madge died? Didn't he have a thumper problem?"

"Just fine. I saw him this morning. He's doing better since the heart attack. He's even out splitting shakes some mornings before breakfast."

"Good to hear it!" said Thelma heartily. "You flyin' them jets yet? We saw one go over the other day and we all said that might be you."

"Not yet. It's still pretty early in my career to be flying those tax burdens. I'm just doing ground school for the basic pilot's license now. I'm actually thinking about getting out of the program altogether."

"Well, that was a quick career. Then we can't talk anymore about how you're going to fly over the house, can we?"

"I guess not. I'm not certain I'm getting out. I'm just not sure about the war anymore. Few people are, I suppose. It's nothing like World War II and Korea, based on the stories I heard when I was growing up. Uncle Henry's stories about Korea and Ben Weeden's stories about the Japanese prison camp he was in were a heck of a lot different than what I hear now about Vietnam. A lot of GIs come back from Southeast Asia and go to school at the state universities. They tell stories, most of which I couldn't or wouldn't repeat to anybody. And now there's this My Lai thing in the newspapers. The scary thing is that My Lai doesn't sound a lot different than some of the tales I've heard from GIs."

The back screen door slammed suddenly and Albert Morton, an old hired ranch hand, walked into the kitchen. A ranch hand for the past twenty years, he was powdered with oat chaff and hay splinters from working in the barn. He banged his hat against the wall, then hung it on a hat hook.

"Look who's come to visit?" Thelma asked him.

Albert looked up from the pantlegs he was brushing with his hands and said after focusing his eyes, "Frankie Ravan." He adjusted the bent, wire-rimmed glasses over his nose and said gently, "I didn't expect ta see ya in the kitchen today. Good ta see ya, Frankie. Good ta see ya."

Stooped from years of hard labor, Albert walked across the kitchen with his arm out like a loose two-by-four. Frank stood up and shook the hand, admiring his thick, bushy gray eyebrows and beard. He shook Frank's hand with diminishing enthusiasm, however, as SueLee gave him a demurring glance. She said, "You should shake yourself off on the porch, Albert, not in the kitchen!"

Albert ignored the comment and immediately began to tell a story. He said to Frank, "That lake ya were askin' me about a few years back, I guess the last time I saw ya."

"Lake?" Frank looked doubtful and raised his hand to his forehead. "Lake? I asked you about a lake?"

"Sure did," replied Albert.

"Water's ready," said SueLee, grabbing her apron and wiping her hands. She reached for the water kettle on the stove, clutched it and placed it on an iron coaster on the table.

"Yes," continued Albert, "the one above Shale Mountain. Ya wanted ta know why it was named Blackmare Lake."

"Oh, yes, I remember now."

"Well, I found out why. It had nothin' ta do with geography. Back in the thirties. . ."

"So why don't you want to be in the service anymore?" interrupted SueLee.

Albert lowered reddened eyes toward the kitchen floor where a puppy was pushing against his leg. He leaned down and pulled it onto his lap by the ears. Noticing a red ribbon in the pup's mouth he pulled it out and laid it over his knee. The puppy had eaten about twenty inches of the ribbon and when Albert pulled it out the pup shuddered as though being tickled all the way down to its stomach.

"It's a long story," replied Frank.

"Yip, yip, yip," went the pup, jumping back down to the floor. SueLee took a broom and swept it out the back screen door where it tumbled down a cascade of concrete steps, then she took the ribbon off Albert's knee.

"I got that ribbon at the county fair last fall for my gooseberry pie," she said. She took the unraveled ribbon and pinned it to a string above the wood cook stove where it could dry.

"In the thirties," said Albert, "there was a mule train that went up the old Shale Mountain trail early in the summer after a heavy winter. . ."

Thelma interrupted, "Do they want you to leave the service, Frank? You didn't do anything you weren't supposed to, did you?"

"Oh, no, nothing like that, Thelma."

"Somehow," said Albert, "one of those mules, a black one, got loose from the rest of the pack train. . ."

SueLee asked, "So you're not going to be in the service at all now?"

"That old mule was black and honery, they used ta say, damned honery it was. It tried ta. . ."

"Ma!" hollered Bern from the back porch. "Pa's coming now."

"Tell him there's coffee!"

Albert reached for an old coffee tin on the table and poured a shot of fresh, raw cream into his coffee mug, his brown finger deep inside the can. Another old dog wandered into the kitchen from a side room and stood in the middle of the floor. A yellow cat walked under the dog's chin and arched upward, rubbing its back with its front paws off the floor. The breaking yellow wave touched the dog's throat, then touched down on all fours. Albert grabbed a spoon out of a round glass bowl on the Lazy Susan. The bowl was next to half a bottle of Alka-Seltzer and two leftover fried trout from breakfast, tails upward.

Albert continued, "It tried ta push its way around one of the other mules in the pack train when it slipped on a loose rock. . ."

"Albert, let Frank tell us why he's going to get out of the service," said SueLee.

Just then little Billy Lucas climbed up a cupboard and tipped over a bowl of batter. SueLee turned in time to see it run down the front of the counter. She yelled at Billy to get down and swatted him on the seat of his pants. He whimpered and wandered into the next room.

"Dillon," said SueLee to her son, "did you get that cow of yours milked?"

"No, Ma."

"Well, get it done now, you hear?"

"So that mule tried ta push its way ta the head of the pack when all of a sudden it slipped and slid down the snow bank all the way ta the lake. . ."

Just then Willard Lucas walked in the back door with Bern who shouted, "Look at Grandpa's trout! They're each at least eighteen inches." Willard, his eyes like shining opals, lifted three rainbow trout into the air. They were still dripping river water.

"Nice'uns, eh? Some of the fightenest I ever seen for rainbows. I thought at first they must be cut-throats. Rainbows usually feel like they're half asleep when you reel 'em in." He walked over and put the trout in the sink, then walked back to see how Thelma was doing. The smell of fish was now everywhere.

"Frank Ravan's come visiting, Willard," she said to him, but Willard didn't hear. "I SAY," she articulated loudly, pointing to her lips so Willard would watch them, "I SAY, Frank Ravan's come to visit!" Then she pointed at Frank.

It finally dawned on Willard that Frank was there in the kitchen. Broad-shouldered for a man of eighty-nine and tall, he walked over to Frank and reached out his hand in greeting, then plummeted into a sagging couch at the edge of the kitchen table.

"That old mule froze ta death in the water before the trail crew had a chance ta think about how ta get it out. . ."

"Please, Albert," said SueLee, "Will you please let Frank tell us why he's not going to be in the service anymore?"

Not wounded, just impeded, Albert looked down at his coffee cup again and reached for a cupcake. A lonely wisp of hair fell over his eyebrow. Frank looked out the back door momentarily and noticed fragments of an old Case combine strewn across grass at the edge of the back yard. Vernon Lucas stepped through the back fence gate.

"Here comes Pa," said Bern, sitting near the doorway.

"Well, Frank, you might as well wait until Vern comes in now before you leave," said SueLee.

Frank stepped toward the door and met Vernon as he ducked in past a rusty crosscut saw hanging from the cobwebbed eaves.

"Frankie! Glad you came by, young fella. We thought you'd be in Vietnam by now," said Vernon. "I must say I'm relieved that you're not. You know how we feel about *that* war."

"Well, it's still early for that," responded Frank.

"How long till supper?" Vernon asked SueLee.

"The roast will be another hour at least."

"You'll join us then, Frank?"

"Well, I can't tonight, but I appreciate the offer."

"Frank's leaving the service, Vern," said SueLee.

"For good? Really? Seems like you just signed up, didn't you?"

"Vern," said Frank. "The war's bothering folks for different reasons. I know a lot of vets who've come back from there and they tell a different story than you might expect. It's not Korea or the Coral Sea, where everything I've read in the ROTC program books is so clear cut."

"Oh, I know that, for sure. The government just took Dirk and threw him over there like a sandbag to rot on a riverbank. I'm one who knows there's something awful wrong about that war. You don't have to convince me of it. I've got a gravestone to prove I know it." Vern got teary-eyed.

A loud clicking noise began in a corner of the kitchen. It sounded like it was coming from behind the wood stove. Then there was a noise like tap water.

"You're not getting kicked out of the service, are you Frank?" asked Vern, suppressing his tears.

"No. It's not like that."

SueLee walked to the back of the stove.

"Did you fail a medical exam?" asked Vern.

"No. It wasn't anything like that either."

"Bern!" hollered SueLee. "Your baby goat is up again. He's piddling the floor."

The clicking noise from little goat hooves began again, followed by a "baaaaa" sound. Bern pulled back a wooden screen and a baby goat tap-danced across the linoleum. The dog got up and sniffed it and the yellow cat passed its tail under its black and brown chin. Bern picked the goat up in her arms and carried it out the back door, her long red hair swirling around the goat's awkward frame.

Walking to a cupboard and pulling down two freshly baked cakes, one lemon-colored with powdered sugar and the other chocolate, SueLee set them on the counter. "Well, Frank, if you're not going to have supper, you may as well have some cake."

"I do still have a sweet tooth," Frank admitted, admiring the creations.

"I have a sweet tooth, too, and it's hurtin' me pretty bad right now!" said Albert.

"All you have left is candy for teeth, Albert," SueLee told him. She looked at Frank and said, "Anything sweet left in the kitchen after hours somehow finds its way into Albert's gullet anyway. Funny how that is."

"So why are you leaving the service?" asked Vernon.

"Well, and I'm sure you probably agree in some ways, I don't think the Vietnam War started for reasons of national defense. I know the general reasoning is that dominos go one by one and the countries around Vietnam are leaning in that direction. There is some truth to that, of course. And it's different than a revolution that starts from the bottom up. I'm just starting to doubt it's likely to produce a good result, for us or for the Vietnamese. At least that's how I'm starting to see it. Mostly, there's a lot wrong with how the war's being conducted. Guys who come back from there say they never felt like they were part of an overall strategy to win. And they say our troops are using a lot of hard drugs and smoking hashish and marijuana before they go into a campaign. It seems wrong and mixed up and I don't know who's to blame. A lot of the Vietnamese are terrified of communism, and they should be. From that perspective we should help them. But our troops don't seem dedicated to that. They're restless and unsure. Sure, I've got a narrow perspective, but it seems more like that all the time. Also, the ghosts of colonialism are everywhere, with the Vietnamese unsure they really are ghosts. In some respects, the French and Americans are just stretching out the old colonialist agenda, so the ideas of freedom and free enterprise aren't believable."

The front door slammed and everyone in the kitchen looked toward the front door. Rud Sleven was standing there in his silver safari helmut, red plaid shirt, shagged black logger pants, and logging boots. Rud was a monstrous, fifty-eight-year-old Czechoslovakian who ran sawmills on the Lucas and O'Seetley properties. He was six-foot-five and husky and took his meals with the families. His wife had died of childbirth with his fourth son after eight years of marriage. His boys were still being raised in foster homes.

Frank used to visit Rud with Percy when Percy needed lumber. He recalled his fenderless tractors with their wheels wrapped with snow-chains like Mexican soldier gunbelts and portable mills run by stand-alone truck diesel engines mounted on huge struts to split logs. Lumber carriage brakes were cabled to rusting train switches and exhaust lines were joined with tomato cans. Rud smoked tin after tin of Prince Albert tobacco rolled single-handedly into wet, twiggy cigarettes.

"Rud, come on in," SueLee said. "Dinner will be ready soon. Frank Ravan, Russell's boy, is here."

"I thought you were in Vietnam," said Rud, a World War II Army veteran.

"Well, I'm probably getting out of the service," Frank said.

"Doesn't surprise me none."

"Why?" asked Frank.

"Cause we shouldn't be there anyway," Rud replied, taking off his flying saucer helmet.

"Really? You're a veteran, too," noted Frank.

"Yes. I think it's a bad deal that war. They's kids getting killed by the hundreds every day and nobody can really explain why. We

watch the evening news before dinner every night and see 'the
dead score' when we should be seeing 'the baseball scores.' It
don't seem reasonable to me. You'd be better off doing something
else until your country *really* needs you. Staying in Vietnam is just
going to give kids a reason to take drugs and dope and space out on
life. My own boys are almost teenagers now and I don't want to
see them end up as cannon fodder, drug addicts, or just a number
on an evening news chalkboard. God knows the heartache that
comes to families like Vern and SueLee's. Dirk would be in his
late-twenties by now. He was about the same age as your brother
Sea when he didn't wake up from his dream."

Vern sat like a brooding stone statue as Rud continued, "That
war over there is different than what we fought in the World Wars.
It's mostly like Korea in a way, but not even that, really. If they
want to be communists, let 'em be, I think. Maybe they'll get tired
of it after a while— when they get hungry— then they'll want their
freedom; then they'll *get it for themselves*. Let them get their own
freedom. We don't have to get it for them. Sure, we could help
em', but I don't think they're ready. The gooks in the South don't
seem to want freedom bad enough, or maybe the Northern gooks
want freedom more, but don't understand Communism. It's
confusing altogether, but it's not our problem. I think it's fine that

you're getting out. A lot of us veterans don't see it the way Nixon does, even though most of us voted for him."

Frank was surprised to hear Rud speak, but realized he had probably been thinking about it for a long time because of his own sons who would be of draft age in a couple of years. "Actually," said Frank, "I'm going to tell my commander that I don't want to stay in the service. They say he'll tell me that I'll regret leaving the service, that I'm just being unduly influenced, that after the government goes ahead and lets me out I'll wish I hadn't asked to be released. They say he'll tell me to keep my thoughts to myself so that I won't 'negatively' affect the good morale of other cadets. He might even see me as a security risk to the program, I suppose. If he does, he could dismiss me, as they say, 'without impunity'."

"What's impunity?" asked SueLee.

"Punishment. They could punish me for wanting out by sending me to Vietnam anyway as an enlistee."

"Well, it'll all work out okay," said SueLee.

"I told Percy and Emelia I'd have supper with them, so I better be going," said Frank, noticing the clock on the wall.

"Take a couple pieces of cake with you," SueLee insisted, reaching for a paper plate. Bern came back into the kitchen and looked flushed, as if she'd been chasing across the yard.

Thelma said, "Give Frank one of those trout. If he don't eat it, I know Percy will."

"Now you know why that lake's named Blackmare," said Albert.

Frank smiled at Albert and said goodbye, then went out the front door toward his car. Bern followed him saying, "We've all missed you, Frankie. Come back soon, real soon. Okay?"

Frank agreed to return soon, getting into his fin-tailed Plymouth as the moon took form in a pale blue sky. The horse that had been in the yard when Frank drove up was now craning its neck inside an oat box at the barn door. It was flipping up the lid with its nose and every time it got a mouthful of oats the lid slammed shut again. Ducks stood in the long shade of a John Deere tractor whose front axle was blocked. A red-winged blackbird streaked toward willows along the Elk Fork River.

That night Frank had a dream that he wrote into his journal the next day:

— Two fish swam in a large fish tank. One fish was big, the other small. The big fish dominated the space in the tank, intimidating the little fish. Suddenly the little fish raced swiftly through the water and bit the big fish in a vital spot. The blood squirted into the water like red ink, clouding the water pink. The little fish retreated and the big fish slid to the bottom of the tank. The little fish then swam about the tank, joyful in its new

experience of freedom. I felt pity for the little fish when it was being bullied, and anger toward the big fish. Then, when I saw the little fish so vicious in that moment, I was horrified at it. Now the little fish is swimming happily and I cannot deny it the joy it might feel. In a way, the big fish killed itself.

HELTER SKELTER

Sheriff Fitz sat down on several cases of canned tomatoes in the back of Morland's Mercantile. He was about to have a glass of blended Canadian Scotch with the boys: Jerry Smit, Mr. Morland, Ray Smollen, and Dick Petrella.

Smollen was the first to note Fitz's swaying manner and discomfort. He seemed off balance, even said he'd been a little dizzy for a day or two. "You don't look too good, Fitz. Are you about to pass out? Sit down. You look a little wobbly."

"Have a drink. It's been a long week," said Morland.

"I'll be fine. Been feeling a little under the weather. Give me a glass of that elixer."

Morland poured and Petrella passed, and Fitz chugged his first portion, then handed the glass back to Morland. "One more will slow down my heart."

Morland obliged. The others all had their first shots as Petrella and Smit lit up filterless Camels. The smoke from cigarettes was thick and blue in the back room. Their lungs expanded to absorb as much nicotine as possible.

The atmosphere in the back room was normal for a late Friday afternoon, except for Fitz feeling out of sorts. "I have to be in Sandy Crossing in an hour to deliver a warrant to that guy staying in the Hewitt cabin. He's wanted for a theft investigation in Boise. Key person in the case or something." Fitz rubbed his left forearm with his right hand and then his bald forehead as he muttered something else with slurred speech. Then he passed his hand back and forth across his forehead one last time so fast that it reminded of a magician's sleight of hand. He got up and turned to go, saying, "I guess I better take care of business."

He wandered through unpacked boxes of freight, some covered with store aprons, on his way to the back door. "See you soon. You hardly had a moment to relax," said Morland. "Ciao!" said Petrella. Smit was puzzled by Fitz's behavior as Smollen held out his glass for another stroke of Morland's hospitality. Said Smit, "Something's wrong there. Fitz ain't himself."

After blowing a string of little smoke rings into the air, Petrella added, "Fitz is still acting a bit out of character. I've seen him this way a few times now. I think he's mixing alcohol with something. He's off balance. That's got to be drugs of some kind."

"He's temperamental these days, too," said Smollen. "That staid old sheriff's manner is gone, as if he never had it."

Morland interjected, "I wouldn't worry about Fitz. He'll swing back to normal soon. I think he's been busy this month. That's the third warrant he's delivered just this week. He's probably tired."

Fitz's cruiser spit several shotgun bursts of gravel behind it as it sped out of the Crawford Nook's alley and onto the highway. He nearly hit Samsins' brown and white collie as he accelerated past the town's population sign that read 128.

"Damned dog!" Fitz muttered. "Every time I come through this town that dog is waiting like a traffic cop. . . tries to race me every time."

Fitz was soon wound like a spring after taking a handful of amphetamines and washing them down with beer and whiskey. The top of his head was hot and his heart felt like a little motor inside his chest, turned on high and buzzing. The cruiser speed was climbing fast and the needle was over 120 mph before he had gone even two miles south of town.

Social change over the last year or two associated with the war in Vietnam and a youth movement grappling with new ideas about drugs was everywhere in the basin. Changes were having diverging effects on several generations.

Fitz had become close to a high school teacher near Bird Ridge who was dealing drugs. They had gone to school together and had grown closer to one another in recent years. The teacher had implored Fitz to understand some of the truants he had taken into custody for smoking marijuana and hashish. "These aren't bad kids. It's a cultural change that all of us need to understand," the friend said. "It's not just adolescents zonked out on drugs. They're all just trying to understand themselves better and trying to find reasons for their country's involvement in a war so far from home, a war that on the surface makes no sense."

Fitz's problem was that he was easily trapped with substance abuse because he was already a heavy drinker. He mistakenly thought he could handle another layer of drugs. It did not take long for his friend to include him in a loop of users, even if Fitz was supposed to be keeping the fox away from the chickens. Fitz had now become a heavy user of various drugs as his friend quietly made his mark as a leading drug dealer in central Idaho. The teacher himself had come back to the states after serving in Saigon and Fitz figured that he should be given a little tolerance on drugs because of his past service to his country.

Toward Fridays Fitz always got heavier on the use, and before too long was mixing uppers and downers with alcohol as a kind of weekend sport. Today he was very high, to the point of hallucinating.

This was a warped way of trying to cope with and understand a new mentality in the country, if it was really that as a driver. Coached by his drug-dealing friend, Fitz frequently told himself that the boys coming back from Vietnam had a right to ease back into society in any way that guaranteed their comfort. Some ex-GIs were pretty messed up mentally and needed a little room to readjust to civilian life, they surmised. The Vietnamese people were somehow responsible for their own mess and they were trying to drag Americans into it unwittingly, Fitz told anyone willing to listen. For Fitz, who was supposed to be enforcing laws, drugs were contributing, evermore frequently, to an apparent haziness in his discrimination.

The cruiser swept south down the main highway in the basin and before twenty minutes Fitz was in the hairpin turns of the lower Elk Fork River canyon. Corner by corner, his car tires squeeled as he intermittently swerved over yellow lines.

Fitz wasn't feeling great but he was high. At one point he imagined his car was several feet above the ground and he fanticized about heading up a hill directly like a chopper to save a little time on the trip to Sandy Crossing just a few miles ahead.

That's when the camper approached and passed him going in the opposite direction, edging slightly off the road to make sure it cleared his car as it crowded the line. As it passed, all Fitz saw in the front of the camper were the frowning faces of a load of Viet Cong, at least a half dozen.

"What the hell?" he shouted. "What the hell? They're not going to speed up this canyon on my watch!"

He hit the brakes on the cruiser and skidded at least 60 feet into a 180-degree turn that ended in gravel at the river bank. He aimed the vehicle north and pressed the accelerator again. Soon he was flying and had the camper in sight.

He could now see an anti-aircraft gun mounted on the top of the camper as it sped around the corners ahead. He anticipated its possible firing.

He roared up behind the camper with siren and lights but the camper just kept driving up the canyon. After several miles he pulled up closely behind the camper and gently bumped its rear bumper.

To this interference the camper slowed and finally pulled over. Fitz raced his car to the front of the vehicle, slammed the gearshift into park, then leapt out the door with his revolver in his right hand and a shotgun in his left. Next, he tucked the shotgun under his arm and with his left hand practically ripped the driver's door off the camper. He yelled at everyone inside to exit and lay down on the ground.

One by one the family members jumped out of the camper and lay down on the pavement face first. "Get down and stay down. Don't move. If anyone moves there will be a bullet to greet you." He then fired two warning shots into the air and one into the asphalt surface of the highway, which spit small fragments tinkling against the metal side of the camper. The Korean mother and two daughters were crying.

About this time an Idaho State Trooper driving south came upon the scene, not knowing anything or expecting anything. The officer stepped out of his car after turning on his own lights and pulling off the road to stop. "Need an assist?" he yelled at Fitz from his window.

"Hell, yes, I caught these Charlies about to fire at me. I've about got it under control."

The trooper carefully looked over the scene and saw something completely different. A Korean man and his wife were sobbing and begging for mercy for their children: two little crying girls and three trembling boys prone on the asphalt. "Don't harm us, Sir. We have done nothing wrong!" the father shrieked. The trooper tried to calm the Koreans.

At the moment the trooper realized Fitz had actually lost his sobriety, Fitz misstepped and fell directly down on his side clutching his chest. He writhed for about twenty-five or thirty seconds, then became still. He had had a massive heart attack.

The trooper quickly got on the radio in Fitz's car; it was closer than the one in his own vehicle. As he requested an ambulance, he

noticed in the front seat two bottles of amphetamines, each half
empty, a partially drained bottle of whiskey and several six-packs
of beer, each with three or four empty cells.

*

Billy Naul was going to find a girl he had once made out with
at a dance in Caldwell. He remembered her address, a trailercourt
in Garden City. He pulled into the "Willow Rest Trailer Court" at
two a.m. and began knocking on doors, but he was unsure which
trailer was hers. He parked his Harley Davidson FLH 1200cc
motorcycle on a patch of lawn, but the trailerhouse next to the
grass was dark and no one stirred to tell him to take the beast
elsewhere. As Billy pounded on doors, he fidgeted with and
adjusted the .38 pistol he had stolen years before and shoved it in
the back of his pants.

"Hey, asshole," he said to an elderly man who answered his
door, "Is Debbie here?"

The man was bald and had a V-shaped face. He answered, "No
need to be rude, Son! Nobody here by that name. Only me. There's
a Debbie June at the end of this row of trailers though." He pointed
down the lighted way toward the Boise River.

"Thanks butthead," said Billy.

"See you, Jerk!" said the man as he slammed his door.

Billy turned and walked another hundred feet down the trailercourt row and up to a porch-shadowed green and white door on a double-wide. He began beating on the door, unconcerned that the eight or nine beers he had already had had made him belligerent.

A young man in his early twenties opened the door. "What the hell do you want?" he asked Billy.

"Is Debbie in?" Billy asked.

"Come back tomorrow. She's sleeping."

"Thank you, but I'll see her tonight. I came all this way from Emmett and I'm not going home without talking with her."

"Get the hell out of here!" said the young man.

"Get out of the way, kid," said Billy. "Debbie! I'm coming in. You haven't called in weeks. Let's go out tonight." Billy pushed his way past the young man and ditched him to the couch with his forearm. He passed through the kitchenette and strode down the center of the trailer toward the back rooms.

The young man got up and pulled a .22 pistol out of a drawer in the kitchenette. He yelled at Billy. "Stop, you son-of-a-bitch, or I'll drop you where you stand!"

Billy looked over his shoulder, then turned and laughed, "What are you going to do with that squirrel gun?"

Just as he got his last word out there were five shots from the .22 and Billy was hit in the chest, back, and head as he turned. He twitched a few times and shouted, "Mother, Jesus! You son of a bitch!" twisting with the impact of the bullets. He fell in the hallway groaning.

The young man immediately got on the phone as Debbie came out of the bedroom in a lavender cotton bathrobe and turned on a hall light.

"Hello, police! There's been a home invasion at 122 Elm in Garden City. Please send someone. A man is down. I had to shoot him. He's still alive. Willow Rest!" The young man set the phone down, slipped on his trousers and put on his Boise Fireman blouse.

Billy Naul died about twenty minutes later in the ambulance on the way to the hospital. The police did not charge the young fireman for defending his home. Debbie said she didn't even remember ever having met Billy.

*

Tom Petrella finished high school with Frankie, then went to work for a logging company that worked steep river drainages in the Salmon River country with cables and helicopters. After his first year of work he became restless over his future. Like other young men his age he also felt some drive to join the military. His veteran father encouraged this, but somehow Tom was not enough inclined to accept the war's nature to go down to the recruiter and sign up. Tom liked living, and dying in war was too much of a prospect for him to get his head or heart around.

On weekends Tom spent time with two of his high school buddies from Weldler's Lake: Curtis Walker and Devin Phelps. The three often drove around the lake and swam and fished wherever there was an open campsight. They were still not old enough to buy beer but were easily able to procure it from Curtis's father who figured they would get it somehow anyway. They often spent Friday or Saturday nights camping and drinking, or boating and drinking when they could get Devin's father to lend them his Chris-Craft Riva inboard motorboat with its Chrysler V-8 for water skiing.

On this Saturday night Curtis and Devin introduced Tom to something new: hashish. Explained Curtis, "You can get it now in Boise or from my guy in Bird Ridge. It's a middle eastern kind of strong tobacco paste, but it's stronger than tobacco. It gives you an incredible high." Tom was intrigued. He'd been a smoker his whole life, so this seemed just a variation on pipe tobacco. Devin took a piece of aluminum foil from his pocket and pressed it into the bowl of a tobacco pipe, then he poked a centered series of tiny holes with a straight pin into the foil base. After this he unfolded another piece of foil and cut a quarter inch cube of the hashish from a larger chunk and placed it in the bottom of the bowl. He lit it, took a breath of the smoke, held it in his lungs, then handed the pipe to Curtis. When the bowl came to Tom he didn't hesitate, immediately breathing the vapor deep into his lungs. He held it there like Devin for at least a half minute before exhaling.

They smoked quietly together for fifteen to twenty minutes, gradually sharing their sensations of euphoria. Tom had never felt anything like this. He closed his eyes momentarily and felt his body leave the car and float above the trees by the lake. He could see ridgetops nearby covered with evening light. He opened his eyes again and sank into his seat in the cab of the truck. He reached for another pipeload of smoke.

Smoking and talking, the three eventually drove out onto the lake road in Tom's fatigue green Chevy truck. They took the road north until it left the shore of the lake and headed into heavy timber. A half hour later they were in the backcountry along the Secesh River, east of Burgdorf. After driving for an hour Tom became thirsty and started drinking beers. By the time the three approached Warren the truck was weaving continuously. "Stop and let me drive," said Devin.

"Oh, I'm fine," Tom assured his companions. But just as they approached a bridge over the Secesh River Tom's left front tire sank into the soft road shoulder. They were going about 40 mph when Tom tried to right the truck and get it back to the center of the road; but as soon as he turned the wheel to the right the truck rolled on its left side and jumped the bank of the river. After the roll the vehicle bounced off a huge hundred-plus cubic foot boulder and slammed headfirst into a two and a half foot thick yellowpine trunk growing on the riverbank.

Tom was dead instantly, impaled on the steering column. Devin was launched through the front window and landed in six feet of river water. He made his way to shore after floundering along in the river current for about a hundred yards. Curtis was also launched into the river but his head was crushed in some rocks in the channel and he died within minutes, actually drowning as his body sunk beneath the surface.

Curtis had some scratches and bruises but managed to pull Devin's body to shore. He couldn't extricate Tom, so left him at the accident scene and walked to Warren where he got help from the Idaho County sheriff who happened to be in town.

COLLEGE '68

Frank loaded a box of books into the back seat of his '57 Plymouth, then ejected an eight-track Steppenwolf cassette from a tape player in the garage. He turned on the radio to news: "South Vietnamese troops pursued enemy regulars in one of the biggest battles of recent weeks. A-hundred-fifty-eight enemy soldiers were killed before South Vietnamese soldiers withdrew. B-52s will step up massive strikes in northern zones in an attempt to slow the steady infiltration of North Vietnamese troops into the South. The South Vietnamese government. . ."

"Such a spectacle!" Frank muttered as he reached over and turned off the radio, then stepped back for a moment to look at the dusty orange car Percy had given him. It was an old Plymouth that had belonged to a third cousin from Oregon he had never seen.

Percy sat in a lawn chair under a yellowpine a hundred feet away. His straw cowboy hat had a few holes in it and a wool scarf fell over the back of his chair, nearly touching the ground. Beyond the old man Frank could see the white rapids of a stretch of Upper Burnt Ruby Creek. On Percy's flanks were yellow and red leaves of alder and aspen and a tall bank of dormant raspberry brambles. Frank imagined that his grandfather was looking at the creek. In fact, Percy was watching a watersnake glide along the grass. The snake came toward Percy as Frank left the garage and walked toward him, then it slithered up Percy's pantleg as Frank came up and stood next to him.

"Did you see that snake go up my pants, Frank? They're coming up from the water now that the frogs are digging into the mud, but he won't find any frogs where he went just now. He'll be back out in no time. A bit more cold weather will put them in the mud, too, for the winter. By the way, gather those last squashes before you leave today. We may get another frost tonight."

"You were teasing me, weren't you, Grandpa, about the snake?"

"No," said Percy. "You watch my pantleg. He'll be back down in a second. He'll have to do a U-turn in the cul-de-sac."

Frank looked at the open pantleg for a few moments, then saw the watersnake slither out on schedule.

"Grandpa! What kind of trick is that? It's a good thing Grandma already passed away because she'd die today if she had to watch that." His grandfather laughed and laughed, remembering how many watersnakes Madge had hacked to bits in her lifetime. "Well, they can't run all the way up your winkie, you know!"

"As a matter of fact, Grandpa, there's a little snake in South America that *can* run up your winkie!"

"Well, I'm glad we live in the mountains where the snakes are smart enough to recognize a dead end."

Frank shook his head at his laughing grandfather and walked over to the porch. He lifted a basket and walked toward the garden, then picked a dozen dark green zucchinis. He moved another lawn chair next to his grandfather's and sat down. Percy took his hat off, then leaned over and resnapped a garter.

"Frank, did I ever tell you about that minister's wife I bit?"

"What do you mean you bit the minister's wife? Were you rabid?"

"Well, we were horsing around in the hot springs many years ago and there was this minister's wife and her two kids in the swimming hole with us. There was also a couple of gals a little older than Deadeye and me, too, and I decided to pull a prank on one of them. I went swimming down real deep then came up underneath one of those gals and took a big soft bite of her hind-end. I didn't break the skin; it was just a playful chomp. I was playing like I supposed otters do.

"When I surfaced, the minister's wife was screaming and her children were wading out to her in a panic saying, 'Are you okay, Mama? Are you okay? What happened?' The gal I thought I bit was twelve or fifteen feet away by then.

"Well, I felt right away that she might not tell them what had happened, but she knew for sure. After I surfaced I said, 'Oh, Ma'am, I'm sorry. That was an accident. Are you okay?'

"She said, 'Oh, yes, yes. I'm fine, just fine.'

"Well, I thought she might go home and tell her husband and he'd be coming over to the home place soon with the sheriff or a gun. I had a moment of panic. Then I noticed a twinkle in her eye and somehow knew she wasn't going to tell another soul on the face of the earth about what had actually happened under the water. Frankly, I think she liked getting a bite in the keester."

"Grandpa. For real?" Frank asked.

"To my dying day I'll say so," responded Percy, laughing loudly.

"You never told Grandma that story, did you?"

"No. She might have heard it from someone else, even Deadeye, but she never said so."

Looking down at Percy's imitation leather slippers Frank said, "I've got to leave today, you know that."

Percy gradually stopped chuckling, then said nothing.

"You know, I've got to leave soon. I'm going back to Seattle."

His grandfather gazed at the creek and a huge tamarack on the far shore. It seemed like several minutes to Frank before Percy finally said, "Look at how thick that tree is. Your father and I cut down three exactly like it so we could build our first house. We got a lot of good lumber out of them before they culled on us. We didn't use them up right away. It was a year or so later that we built a decent mill."

"Where was that first mill?"

"In the lodgepole around the base of chimney rock, near where you and Sea buried the slaughtered deer."

"I knew of an old mill by the white barn, but I didn't know you had one near Deadeye's old road."

"It was so long ago now you can't see any evidence of its ever having been there. We tore out the old timbers and burned them."

"I'll be home the first chance I get. I may have to take up logging for a while to earn money for school. If they let me out of the service I won't have a scholarship anymore."

"They won't bother you about it, Frank. I expect there's a whole lot of boys your age trying to avoid the war right now. It's not making a lot of sense to people and it's not like the other wars we've fought. It doesn't feel like patriotism is driving our participation. There's not a common motive for everyone. Just remember: this is home, your home. There's no place like it. Spend as much time here as you can until you have to move on."

"What do you mean avoiding the war right now?"

"Well, you seem to be trying to figure things out, whether the war's a good thing to be involved in or not. I can't help you. I don't know much about the service life. The draft dodgers sure aren't doing anybody any good. As I see it, most of them are scared. I've heard a lot of them interviewed on television and they're just afraid and confused. Some of them are insulting and use filthy language. It's hard to believe one generation has so many young men like that. I suppose in a way we all have to take some responsibility for it."

Frank and Percy both felt the silence. There was only the purling creek's murmur beyond the grass. Frank was going over his checklist: clothes boxes, suitcase, camera, track satchel, canned fruit, a case of motor oil for the trip, stop and see Brid in Lewiston.

"There," said Percy, pointing toward the Notch. "Another flock of honkers."

The two watched the V of geese elongate raggedly until it passed over the creek and eastward toward the oat fields in the Notch.

"I'll be back again soon, Grandfather. I'm worried about that car though. It's burning so much oil."

"Yeah, I figured it would. The block might have a hairline crack. It won't last more than another few thousand miles. When you get to Seattle, sell it to somebody for a hundred dollars and I'll get you another one. You might have to go down to Oregon to pick it up though. Your cousins down there always have more used cars than they can sell. I could buy you one at cost every year for the rest of your life and it wouldn't pinch their profits."

"That'd be great. I appreciate the help."

Percy put his hands to his neck and wrapped the scarf tighter. He was not scowling, but Frank was certain he would not acknowledge his leaving. Frank was thinking about the drive ahead and pilot ground training. He imagined himself flying over the ranch someday and seeing his grandfather sitting in his chair near the creek. He thought of Bridget. Would he marry her and live on the ranch?

"I'm going now, Grandfather," he said, sensing how strongly Percy resented his going. Percy said nothing, though Frank noticed his right hand quiver. The resentment was melting.

Frank put his hand on Percy's shoulder, then kissed his cheek. The old man reached up and wiped a tear out of his eye. He said to Frank, "See you soon. Don't do anything I wouldn't do. Do anything I would."

"Don't worry, Grandpa. I won't get into much trouble." As Frank spoke he stood up and walked toward the Plymouth. He watched Percy's back as he pulled out of the driveway: the image of a solitary rancher attached to the earth by his morals and hard work.

*

At the arts and crafts gallery he met Beullah, his mother's business partner, who was in a distracted capitalist mood. Beullah was always trying to make money, but could never make enough to sustain any of the businesses she started. She was singing to herself as Frank walked in, silly lyrics to the effect of, "When I was a little boy I used to sleep a lot. When I was a little girl I used to dream a lot. When I was a little calf I used to play a lot. . . "

Seeing Frank she said, "If these displays sell anything, we're going to get in a whole line of larger plastics. There's plenty of room to store them in the basement. We don't need all that room down there for paintings. Plus, there's a new hanging system I want to put in soon. You can use it to hang ten times the normal number of paintings on any gallery wall. It's a series of cables and clamps that rotate when you pull on a cord like the ones on a Venetian blind, but they go sideways. It's very clever. Here, I'll show you a picture of it."

Frank, recognizing her as the reliant planner, said, "Oh, don't bother. I get the idea. It sounds great. I'm sure it will work fine. Mother says you'll be busy through fall this year, that more people than ever are expected in Weldler's Lake for Octoberfest."

"Oh, we're never sure of anything, Frank. Customers are fickle. There have been more of them in this year overall, but you never know how long a good streak will go. And a beer fest isn't everything. We could have two feet of snow by the end of October anyway!"

Beullah had short brown hair and wore turquoise and silver earrings. Her cheeks were not chubby, but smooth and always glinting like porcelain under light. Frank imagined her as a young woman at her parents' ranch in New Mexico, walking her horse along a corral fence. Inside her childhood home Frank visualized a painting over the family fireplace: oil on canvas of a desert ranch home; the sky was barely blue and there were desert flowers and cacti everywhere. The flowers were bent by a light breeze. The feeling was warm, arid, lonely, heartache beautiful.

"So, you're going back to college today?" she asked.

"Yes. Oh yes. I have everything packed. I'll make it to Lewiston before dark. My only worry is how much motor oil my car drinks. Sometimes I feel like I'm driving a defoliation rig for the county."

Beullah chuckled and reached for a box under the counter. "Did you see Brid when she was home? She was here, I heard."

"No, I missed her. I'm going to try and see her this evening in Lewiston."

As they were talking, Emelia came in the side door.

Frank turned toward her as she walked up beside him, gray hair plaited into a ponytail. Unlike his grandfather, however, whom she had lived with and taken care of since his grandmother Madge had died a year earlier, she did not act offended at his going away to college. Instead, there was a proud sadness in her eyes. It was not well hidden as she dropped a package onto the shop counter and went toward the cash register.

"I have a pie here for you and some sandwiches for the trip." She lifted a large brown bag from under the cash register where Beullah had placed it. "Thanks, Beullah, for taking it out of the fridge. She remembered, Frankie, that you love your pie at room temperature. We both thought you might want a piece before you hit the road."

Frank again overheard Beullah singing under her breath what he thought was: "When I was a little boy I used to sleep a lot. When I was a little girl I used to dream a lot. When I was a little calf I used to play a lot. . . "

"What's that you're singing, Beullah? It sounds rather highlandish."

"It's just something my Mama and Daddy used to sing me when I was a little girl. They'd exchange the word boy with the word girl so the boy dreamed sometimes and the girl slept, depending on what mood they were in and what they wanted me to think about as I fell asleep. It was a game. The calf was always playing, and it was sometimes a lamb. You get the drift."

Several days later Frank wrote the following dream into his journal:

— I was sleeping in front of the living room couch. It was warm; there was a warm orange fire popping in the fireplace. The sparks made a tinkling sound when they hit the screen. Outside the room there was a moon, and the shadows of a couple of raccoons crawled along maple and spruce branches. I floated to the top of the room, then continued upward through the roof until I was several hundred feet over the house looking toward Matthews Ridge. The valley below was cold and midnight blue.

⁂

As he was driving out of town Frank ran into his friend Don who was driving his father's old Chrysler Imperial. The car was wellknown in the county because it had been repainted, but the paint job hadn't held. The paint had gradually peeled away, giving the car a worn lizard skin look. They pulled over to opposite sides of the highway and got out to talk. Frank walked over to Don.

"So what's the status on the draft?" Frank yelled at him.

"I got word a couple of days ago. I'm probably going into the Marines. I'll be drafted by January, I figure. My number came up too low, but I could enlist and do less time."

"Don, that sounds like you're going to prison."

"I don't mind going; I just want to keep it as short as possible. A lot of guys are getting blown away toward the end of their duty. There's such bad luck over there. And it seems that the odds of dying are the highest toward the end."

The sun was setting and the afternoon light was a ghostly shade of yellow, one Frank was seeing for the first time. The faint smokiness in the air from a nearby forest fire coated the whole mountain range with a pale lemon-colored phosphorescence. Don lit a cigarette.

"Can you keep your sanity in the Marines? It's the bottom of the pile and there's pressure all the time. They have the highest casualty figures."

"It's got to be the Marines, Frank. It's a family thing."

"But they're so driven, always trying to prove that they're the only capable fighters in the theater. They take on more than their fair share of work, for sure. Why not join the National Guard?"

"The Guard? Why didn't you join the Guard? And do what? Keep the enemy from attacking Boise, Idaho? Come on, Frank. We all know that the Marines are the best fighters in the Pacific Fleet. Damn the torpedoes, full speed ahead for me; it's going to be the Corps. You know that."

"Well, I guess it's stupid to talk otherwise with you. You're a brave man, Don."

"Who knows what I'll do in a war? I sure don't. Maybe I'll go nuts and wander off into the jungle forever. Maybe I'll end up in a bamboo torture chamber somewhere. Who knows? If anyone thinks that I can soldier right though, you do. I'm worth the risk, I'd say. I'm more content than you are most of the time about whatever's going to happen. I think I can handle it. I'm more likely to be able to handle it than many guys."

"Why do you say that?"

"Because I'll be content just to get done with it in the time it takes, then I'll get on with my life. I'll do it, then walk away from it. I won't think too much about it until it's over. It's one advantage I have over you, Frank. You're never really content or happy, are you? You have to mull things to death. This war has made you more serious and morose than ever. All you do nowadays is try to figure out why it's occurring."

"I don't follow you, Don. People can be happy and still take things seriously."

"Oh, sure, buddy. I'm convinced. Look at you. Who are you trying to convince with that horse face?" Don laughed and took a drag from his cigarette.

"I don't understand. Sometimes you really bug me." Frank knew his friend thought him overly serious. He didn't know how not to be. It seemed that everything needed explanation and justification.

"You don't want to understand what I'm saying. Frank, you're glum, glum over death. Death's got you in its claws. It's one of the most obvious things I've ever seen: your Indian sign. You used to joke around all the time. Even Brid says so these days. She's told me how upset you've made her with your constant talk about death and Vietnam and commitment and patriotism. I think she just wants to get the hell away from you these days."

"Stuff it, Don! What business is it of yours how she feels? You haven't had death licking around your family door yet. Wait till it bites you. I know your philosophy: Life is a maze and no route ever gets us out. No matter how long we're in the labyrinth, we can only expect dead-ends. We choose them and go on with life, turn around, then go into another dead-end, and another. What the hell is that but some kind of sick worship of the inevitable and stupid? Be happy and cheat death as long as you can?"

"Well, that's a bit of caricature, don't you think? But it's not half bad," said Don. "I never thought of it quite like that, but hey, maybe you're right-on, man. That might well be me. It's as good of an axiom as I've heard in a while. See, Frank, I learned something from geometry class. An axiom is a self-evident proposition that you can use to study the consequences that follow. Does that ring a bell?

"Daniels, third period?"

"Of course. We make the best of our lives and take the end when it comes. Your trouble is that you're always anticipating the sequence of everything. Just relax about sequence and go with the flow. What happens is going to happen and it'll lead to other happenings. You'd be a lot happier if you moved along with everything that happens to you instead of fight it and get troubled over it.

"So, I guess that's fate, is it not?"

"Maybe," acknowledged Frank. "If anybody knows. What did you mean about sequence though? It seems to me that geometry has a lot to do with sequence, too."

"Well, you made a big decision and jumped into the military, right? You were sure it was the right thing to do. You so needed to do the right thing, as you always do. But then you realized you 'got it wrong' doing it, so you agonized over the fact that you didn't know enough in the first place to make a good decision. Now, you're going to go back on it if you can. If anything, you think life is supposed to be sequential. It ain't. It's all backwards and inside out and wrong because of any number of reasons. That's the norm. It's what's typical. But for you, any time you do the right thing, it could be the wrong thing, but you'll never know it's the wrong decision until you make it. My view is that when you find out too late you ought to live with it anyway."

"Well, that seems true, for the most part, I suppose. Decisions tear me apart. That's just how I'm wired."

"See, you know I'm right; I'm your alter ego. I've always been your alter ego. It's my job. So why don't you lighten up on yourself? If I got over there to Vietnam and started thinking I should have dodged the draft and become a fisherman in the Canadian Maritimes, what good would it do me? I could get real depressed about it. Jesus H., what good would that do? You've got to relax wherever you are, whatever you're doing."

"You're going to make a great pot smoker, Don. But actually, I think you damn well brood about it as much as I do. You just don't see decisions in terms of results. I am hung up on that; I'll give you that. I've got to imagine admirable or ignoble results in order to make a decision in the first place. I admit, I like to imagine I'm always making good, right decisions that aren't going to come back on me. A fear of discomfort or pain, maybe."

"You're really mixed up, Frank, if you don't mind me saying so. Don't make light of me just because I'm trying to help you see something about Brid either. She couldn't give a damn about your convoluted decision-making processes. It's not fair of you to want or need her to. You've made her really uneasy with all the 'big military choices' you've chosen to make."

"What the hell business is it of yours how it affects her?"

"I'm your friend, and her friend."

"Really? Okay, maybe I'm missing the point. Maybe I do think about death more than you, or talk about it more anyway. And maybe I'm caught in this eddy of 'doing the right thing or not being able to'."

"That's not what I'm saying. It's just not good to express it so much. Keep it inside a little; privatize it. Women can't handle as much bald honesty as we can; particularly when they think it might ruin every hope they have. They want devotion, love, babies, homes, paychecks, security. They can't imagine going off to fight somebody with guns and bullets and bombers and napalm."

"So we're supposed to be fakers?"

"That's not what I'm saying either. You can be honest and still keep things to yourself and brood about them when you're alone. Meanwhile, you're giving the world a good face, an honest face."

"A happy face?"

"Frank. I'm not trying to be a jerk."

"But you are one. Okay, I'll take the advice. Enough said. Just shut up about Brid. That's my problem, if there is one."

Don winked and said, "I know you're with me on this. It's not easy on either one of us. Military decisions are screwing our whole generation up. The war has kind of taken over our lives, and it's not even a part of anything we know. It's kind of hit us all with an unfamiliarity that is unkind. It's an imitation of life.

"Frank, we don't really know shit about war, but it's around us every day. It's words. It's ideas. It's not even something we can touch except through photographs. It's like going to Miami when nobody in the valley has ever been there before. It's exotic, far away, dangerous, alluring. It's dope and shooting and whores and ideas." Don started up another cigarette after flicking the butt of his last one into a mud puddle beside the road. A loaded logging truck rolled past and a blast of wind hit them both.

"Don, if either of us goes over there, there's a good chance we'll die without any sense of why we were there. Our dying would be an accident, not even the result of having tried our best on any kind of mission. It seems that too many guys in Vietnam die from simple carelessness, heedlessness, or recklessness. Dirk Lucas was blown to bits because the guards at his base were smoking opium the night he was killed instead of watching the perimeter for mortar launchers."

"I didn't know that, Frank." Don took a long drag on his cigarette and scowled. To Frank it seemed like feigned concern, but he did not comment. Sometimes Don led him on with melodrama; other times the drama was real. He could not read him today.

"Well, that's what Rud Sleven says. I couldn't get it out of Vern. Look, the Army and the Marines are demoralized and disorganized. The war has never been planned effectively, and the mistakes never get sorted out so they happen again. They happen over and over and over like television serial reruns. Every so often the U.S. Government dumps more soldiers into the sewer and they go spinning down the jungle pipes to hell."

"Listen to us; a couple of roadside philosophers. You're right, but it's our fault, Frank. We're signing up. Aren't we the ones responsible for it because we won't say no? After all, we're the ones agreeing to charge off to cut throats, throw grenades, and drop bombs in the name of some twisted freedom ideas."

"Well, I'm going to pull the plug. I don't think I can go through with it the way it seems I have to. It's too crazy over there right now. We could possibly have won the war a few years ago, but it's not going to happen now. No one is taking any responsibility for the war, but it's worse than negligence. Now it's just ignorance. It's been nearly thirty years since fresh American blood was shed in a war. People have forgotten what it's like to invite death to the dinner table every evening. After a while we start to think death might not be that bad a guest."

"After a while, yeah," Don agreed. He stepped back from his Chrysler and zipped up his coat jacket. A muscrat wandered out of some cattails and broke into a canter across the road, then dove into a pool behind a ditch dam. "If you blinked, Frank, you just missed a scrat dive."

"I saw it. Look, if you go to Nam you'll be doing what that muscrat does every day, probably several times a day. I guess WW II was the last big real one, real in the sense of having much meaning for freedom."

"We all believe that, Frank, under the surface. And Korea was nothing, really, I don't think. It's kind of a big blank in most people's minds. When a guy went off to fight in Korea he was just gone for a long while, like going to South America or the Arctic to explore. People who were around during Korea say there was no media hype like Vietnam, and certainly no high casualty rates. There was no dinnertime news and death counts. I remember going to a cemetary in Caldwell once with my father and we were both surprised to see a tombstone dedicated to the death of a soldier who fought in Korea. Really, I don't think that war touched most people."

"I guess that's true," Frank agreed, adding, "I heard my grandfather and Deadeye talk about it a few times. I think Deadeye knew someone who served in Korea before a Congressman lobbied on behalf of his family to let him come home to plow a field for a crop."

Don took another drag on his cigarette. "I'll be here till January I think. Then I'll probably be drafted. I've got to get to work. You take care of yourself."

"I'm glad I ran into you, Don. I stopped at the ranch house and no one was around."

"I'll see you. Good luck."

"I love you. Yeah, Yeah, Yeah, Yeah, Yeahhhh!"

*

Brid O'Seetley had grown up at the hot springs near Upper Burnt Ruby Creek Notch. Her mother moved there after Brid's uncle John O'Seetley passed away in 1961. At thirteen she was a dark Irish beauty with roan-brown eyes and freckles, and a naturally imperious but intelligent temperament that Frank grew to love. A plumpness in her cheeks— when she had first come to the mountains— was now all but gone and what remained were pillowy lips and two thin shadows that balanced along her smile like feline whiskers. Frank especially liked Brid's gait. She always kept her head up and had the posture of a drum major. When she was moving toward him he felt her sense of absolute purpose.

Brid stayed with an aunt in California during her early school years, but spent summers on the Upper Burnt Ruby with her mother. Eventually, she came to live with her mother in the mountains and she and Frank went to high school together. They dated frequently and used every opportunity to talk, pet, do chores and homework together.

When at the O'Seetley place, she was never far away from Frank, who soon forgot about the many boys in California who had liked her. One followed her to Idaho to visit a few months after she moved there permanently in her last year of high school, but he only stayed for a week at the O'Seetleys and was never seen again. Frank tried to forget about the brief rivalry, but occasionally reproached Brid for attracting the boy to the mountains. She claimed innocence in the situation and always reaffirmed her loyalty to Frank.

In the end, California was another world, another life. And Frank did his best to pretend it did not exist. He hoped that Brid would stay in the mountains and that they would have their day in the sun to grow into a committed couple.

Every June before she moved to the high country Frank anxiously awaited her arrival when, wearing new summer clothes and a brightly colored scarf over short black hair, she always stepped out of the family car at her uncle's ranch and greeted him with a joyous smile and embrace. He always met her there the day she arrived. He could think of doing nothing else on the day she was to arrive.

When Frank was not working, going to school, or working out for the cross country team, he and Brid were hiking, swimming, skiing, running, doing farm work, discussing life, or just learning how to please one another with a kiss or touch. They talked about everything: school courses, college plans, sports, ranching and farming, family, religion and philosophy, ideas about beauty. They talked about their growing love for one another, about their possible future together in the Northwest, somewhere away from it all in Washington, Idaho or Montana, and about the feud John O'Seetley and Percy had conducted over the years over water rights. Frank jokingly called Brid 'McCoy' and she called him 'Hatfield'.

The best times Frank could remember with Brid were spent chasing deer and grouse through deadfall and eating sandwiches and drinking stream water in the hot sun. After going off into the woods together for whole afternoons they often returned to the hot springs nearby, quickly changed in a bungalow by the pond, and plunged off a short wooden dock into its womblike warmth.

Together there they would swim and splash and lounge without a care in the world, even when other swimmers showed up to enjoy the warm baths.

*

Frank found Brid at her rooming house in Lewiston later that day; she was reclining in a large wicker chair on the porch and reading the biography of a U.N. diplomat. The weather was warm and foul odors from the pulp mill along the Clearwater River saturated the air. A Lapwai Indian peddler with apples, peaches, and necterines was parked next to the driveway, his sign propped against a stump on the lawn of the house.

"Hi Hatfield!" Brid shouted, delighted to see him. She ran down the walkway and kissed him and he told her he could stay for several hours before continuing on to Seattle.

"Let's walk along the river," Frank suggested, feeling a powerful energy of love as he took her hand and looked closely at her red and white-checked skirt that looked like it had found its way out of an Italian eatery.

"I have to lock up the house. Mrs. Johnson is not here and I told her I'd look after everything. She's gone to a funeral in Grangeville. She's spending the night."

"Does she live here by herself?"

"Well, except for me. Her husband died five or six years ago. There's another vacant room on the second floor. Her sister comes and stays with her in the winter sometimes. I don't know if she will this year."

After letting Brid lock the rooming house door, Frank put his arm around her waist. "That's not enough for me. I need you to hold me, Frank, like you're not going away. I wish I could see you more. There's a willow grove down by the river and a long bench. Come on, I'll take you there." The sun was radiant as they walked down the sidewalk. The white siding of the rooming house was blindingly bright and hot with the last evening sunshine. Frank recalled O'Seetley's off-white house that hadn't been painted in forty years before Brid's mother moved to the ranch. They stepped slowly along an overpass on the main street and walked toward a grove by the river. Brid wore a low-cut, unironed sleeveless blouse above her skirt and had her hair pinned up. Frank had on blue bellbottoms and a red and black flannel shirt. As they walked, he kept one hand on the coolness of her shoulder.

"So you've started reading biographies?" he asked.

"I saw it at the library. This man lived an unfulfilled life. I think that's why I picked it up. I wanted to know the frustration of that, going along in life unable to grasp what one really wants. It seemed kind of melancholy, but it is written well."

"Do you think your life will be unfulfilled? That you'll miss your mark?"

"I don't know, maybe. What really matters is that you're going away the very day you came to see me."

"You're leaving, too, soon, and that will be for months."

"I know. I don't really want to go."

Frank was unable to make sense of the words Brid spoke. She was saying she didn't want to go, yet she was going to Spain. He was excited by the touch of her, yet annoyed by the game they played about whose affections were strongest. He was also caught up in what was ahead of him and his ego was stranded. Everything was going to change soon, immediately, too fast. New things he wanted awaited just days away. He did not think much about the inevitable changes ahead for her. When he saw her next it would be like seeing her after just another college event, an educational excursion. She would have the same happy, clear brown eyes. She would be ready to give him her undivided attention as she usually did. He would wonder about any differences.

"I'm just on the eastern side of Washington and you're on the western side. We're not that far apart," Frank assured her.

"Well, we will be far away. Spain is a long way away."

"Once you're back from Spain we'll only be four or five hours apart. Spain is just an interval; then we can travel back and forth again to see each other whenever we want over the next few years. Then college will be over and we can settle down to a family life."

"We're going to change even more than we have in just the last year apart, Frank; of course, we won't see the changes until next time we're together. Or in our letters: you'll say something that will terrify me with its significance, or you won't understand something I say. It might be hard this next time. How will we handle surprises? You may fall in love with someone else and then I'll have to make a new life as a result. I know you could. Couldn't we find an alternative? Why don't you come to Spain with me?"

"That sounds impractical, Brid. My interests are different than yours. And I'm on a partial scholarship; I can't walk away from that. It just won't happen. I'm not going to find anyone. I'm not looking. You must know that. Why would I? You know I love you. You're right for me. You can depend on it. That won't change even when we change. We just have to sort some things out on our own and get ready to settle down to the quiet, country life we both want. Don't we?"

"Well, yes, but that sounds flowery and sedentary, even boring the way you say it. What if you discover you really want something very different than living with me the rest of your life?"

Frank, of course, did not understand that Brid was really giving him a warning about herself. He just continued, "I'm sure of what I want. I'm kind of kidding when I refer to the country life. We'll need good jobs or professions so we can support our family. And more than anything else I want a family with you. I think we can sort it out. It will unfold okay."

"I know. . . I wish we were close enough to go up by the creek right now to see if there are any fish spawning. I'd like that— to go there whenever we choose— not just when we happen to be together back at the Notch. I need a fantasy getaway place that's right here with us, something we can just slip into, like a gated rose garden or park."

"I know what you mean, I really do. That would be liberating and calming."

As they walked along the street Frank remembered the last summer hike they had taken to Crowfly Lake. He had dived into the cold sapphire water and swum below the surface for forty or fifty feet while holding his breath. When he surfaced, his skin felt as if it had been burned with ice. The wind blew water like little webs of awn into his face and he was as happy as it was possible to be. Brid stayed on a rock in the sun, unwilling to jump into the cold lake. She just sat there watching him, under spruce trees towering along the shore. After drying off on the rock, Frank took Brid by the hand and they ran the trail around the lake. On their way back down the main trail to the Ravan ranch they ran into Biscuit Laudon, the county ditchrider, who was on his way to the lake to fish.

After passing him that day Frank had said to Brid, "Now there's a peaceful, educated man. After he got his degree from Yale College he came out here to settle down and live a solitary scholar's life. All he does is read books and ride horses all day, every day. And he is always eating his giant biscuits with raw vegetables from his garden."

She had responded, "It that your ideal, Frank? Would you like to be on your own in the mountains to ride and read, to wander and dream and eat vittles out of a saddlebag?"

In turn, Frank had said, "Oh, I don't think so; but I've always admired Biscuit. He meditates with seriousness and knows himself.

He is unpretentious and unusual. He can leave his cares and float into the night on a silver cord."

"Romantic?"

"Not really. I wouldn't say he's romantic. You've seen him. You know he's not romantic. He could bathe more and trim his hair!"

"Maybe that's not the right word. More like esoteric or maybe even lost in time. He seems like he's a hundred years old, like he got lost on the way to the Civil War."

"Yes. That's it. Lost in time. He belongs to no one and has nowhere to go. He's always pleased with life. I think those are great qualities. Nobody else I know has those together. My grandfather and your uncle. . . they were tied to place more than they should have been. Biscuit was more like the Indians that used to traverse the forest along Matthews Ridge every fall. There was magic and beauty, elusiveness, wonder and no connection to the homestead. They passed through and time itself passed. They had what they had and didn't seem dissatisfied. He just doesn't share an Indian's perplexity at what was going on."

Back in Lewiston he heard Brid say, "I heard from the scholarship fund, Frank. They offered me $2,000 toward the three months of study in the Pyrenees this winter."

"That's great. Then it was worth taking the exams?"

"Yes, but I'll miss you so much."

"Hey, it's only three months, remember. I'll be here in Washington waiting for you."

"You want me to go, don't you, Frank?"

"Of course I do."

"I wanted to spend December, January, and February with you. They won't let me use the funds in the summer, at the end of the school year, when I'd rather go."

"The months will fly, Brid. I'll be here. I'll write to you."

"I'll miss you so much. I guess it'll be okay."

"Sure it will be, and I'll see you soon anyway when you come hunting with Don and me."

"You have to write me this fall, long letters, and you have to come see me in Lewiston whenever you can. It's so lonely here. I don't want to be this alone all the time. I don't have as many friends as you have. You're gregarious. I tend to spend too much time alone. You know everybody. You get to know people easily and quickly. I spend a lot of time alone and I don't really like it. It just seems to have to be that way with me."

The conversation continued in this manner for another hour or two until each was certain of the other's loyalty. They embraced, closed their eyes, and traveled to the creek. They saw redfish swimming gently in pools and listened to the flow of the river as they touched. When they got cold they went back to Brid's room and got a wool blanket. Back at the grove they lay in each other's arms until they gradually fell asleep. As light broke at five a.m. they awakened and walked back to Brid's room and slept another hour, then Frank awoke and walked Brid to his car.

He kissed his girl goodbye, got into the Plymouth and drove away. She walked up and stood on the porch of the rooming house where, in his rearview mirror, he could see her sitting down on the steps by herself. He did not fully realize that she felt lonelier than ever.

The next evening Frank wrote this dream into his journal:

— Brid and I held each other for hours. We dove into a clear lake and swam underwater with our eyes open, looking at fish and plants and the sun flashing unevenly through the roof of water. Below we could see shafts of sunlight reflecting off huge monoliths of green glass. I placed my fingers high on her hips and felt chilled contours beneath the swimsuit fabric. I peeled the swimsuit off slowly and felt her icy skin. She didn't seem able to feel my touch.

A CURIOUS STATE

The Indian crew that past summer had come from Gallup, New Mexico: three sixteen-year-old Navajos named Clarence, Rick, and Pete. They worked for the logging company piling brush, hired under a youth employment program to assist families on reservations. They kept Frank, who played the role of their supervisor, busy all summer, especially in the evenings when he was supposed to be off-duty. The logging company housed the crew in a bunkhouse at the logging camp and provided no transportation for them for travel to town.

The owner of the company figured that if he could keep them out of Crawford's Nook or Weldler's Lake taverns he could keep them away from alcohol and trouble. The taverns, of course, weren't supposed to serve juveniles, but anyone knew that a youth, especially young Indians in Idaho, Montana, or Oregon who wanted booze badly enough, could get it whenever they wanted. Several disparate factors merged to create the likelihood that young Indians would get into trouble with alcohol: their weakness for strong drink, plain old youthful indulgence, and white social disdain for Indians which subtly encouraged their dereliction.

Although the logging camp was seventeen miles from Weldler's Lake, the Indian crew soon learned that they could be at the bars by about eleven p.m. They started walking as soon as they were off work about five or six p.m. After walking five or six miles from camp they could hitchhike any remaining distance to town with ranchers who lived along the farm-to-market roads.

Frank took his first call from the local sheriff a week after the crew began work. A local had bought a case of beer for them and they had gotten drunk and disorderly outside of a bar in Weldler's Lake. They were arrested after breaking a street light with a rock.

After the sheriff called the logging company owner, the owner asked Frank to pick up the crew from jail and drive them back to camp.

A second incident with drugs occurred a couple of weeks later at the camp. Rick and Pete approached Frank and told him that Clarence had passed out in the paint shack. "What the hell is he doing in the paint shack?" Frank asked.

Rick, who always wore a gray and white feather dangling from a silver chain on his neck, replied, "We couldn't get no booze. Have none for many nights. Clarence breathed paint. He's in the paint shed."

"So, Rick, are you telling me he went in there to sniff paint because he couldn't get a beer?" Frank asked. Rick just stared at him and said something in Navajo to Pete.

As Frank impatiently walked toward the paint shack, he could see one of Clarence's boots sticking out the cracked shed door. "Why didn't you at least drag him out of there?" he asked Pete and Rick as he grabbed Clarence's leg by himself and began pulling.

The Indians just stared at him. Finally Rick said with a smirk, "He was soooo happy."

Clarence's face was olive-colored and he was as still as death by the time Frank got him into the fresh air. Rick and Pete walked down to a nearby creek, peeled off their tee-shirts and soaked them with cold water, then came back and squeezed them over Clarence's face. Frank, noting that they had obviously had some experience waking up their inebriated brothers, checked for Clarence's pulse, then called the U.S. Forest Service dispatcher on his radio. He assured the dispatcher, once it became clear that the cold water would not rouse Clarence, that he looked pretty dead and needed emergency medical assistance. He said to the dispatcher, "Yes, the boy has a pulse, but it's very weak. I think you've got to launch that rescue bird NOW."

She responded, "We'll have a chopper there in twenty minutes. If he's been smelling lead paint fumes, the only thing that'll save him is getting him some pure oxygen. We'll fly him out to the hospital immediately, but we'll have oxygen on board and an EMT. I'll radio the chopper. Be ready for it. Wrap him in blankets."

In a short while, a big helicopter broke the wilderness calm and dropped over a crest of a long green mountain above the logging camp. It landed at the camp, providing a spectacular event for the Indian crew. Later they told Frank that they had never seen, from such close proximity, a helicopter whip up the air with such thunderous force. After the flying machine settled on the ground, they all trundled Clarence, mummified in green blankets, aboard the chopper. Then, making a deafening buzz, it leapt into the air and shot back up the mountain wall toward the hospital in Weldler's Lake.

It was a mere twenty-four hours later when a Forest Service ranger dropped Clarence back off at the logging camp. His speedy recovery led to a couple of quiet, uneventful days, but too little excitement soon made the Indian crew restless again.

Soon they had planned their own private rodeo, targeting the use of stock from a nearby ranch north of O'Seetley's. Pete and Clarence, who had won gold and silver rodeo belt buckles, respectively, in New Mexico state's junior rodeo championships, had been yearning for a chance to ride the stock horses and mules from the nearby spread. The animals had caught their attention every time they had driven past in a logging company vehicle. They figured that the ranch house was abandoned because no one was ever around the out-buildings or fields where a dozen horses and mules grazed serenely.

The Navajos conducted their stock rodeo one evening in a high, lodgepole corral on the backside of a dilapidated barn. The rodeo did not last long, however, because a ranch hand spotted the trouble soon after it began. When he rode up to the barn in his pickup truck the Indians were riding the mules bareback. As the animals were pack stock instead of riding stock, the Indians traumatized them by leaping onto their backs and riding them around the corral bareback. To the animals it must have seemed barbaric. In the stirring pot of panic and dust, one of the mules— frightened out of its wits— did a barrel-roll over a high fence and cut its shoulder. Another one peeled a flap of hide away from its nose like a long, leather shoe tongue after running full speed, head-on into a closed barbed wire gate at one end of the corral.

Arriving on the scene, the hired man quickly fired a couple of shots into the air with his rifle and instructed the Indians to get away from the animals. After he lined them up beside the barn where they thought they would be shot, he had his son walk to the ranch house and call the logging company owner to tell him to come and get his crew.

When Frank drove up to pick up his charges he saw that the hand still had his rifle cocked and at his hips. The Indians, chewing timothy stems, were sitting on the ground next to a pile of house logs and barbed wire spools. "We'll send you the veterinarian and blacksmith bills!" the hand yelled to Frank as he left to do the evening irrigating.

Frank took the crew back to camp and the owner had a talk with them, but they, of course, acted as if they didn't understand anything he said. To Frank the lecture seemed wholly ineffective because Pete, Rick, and Clarence sat there in front of the boss eating sandwiches instead of listening, sandwiches of white bread soggy with chopped jalapeno peppers and Tabasco Sauce.

When Frank drove into the camp the next morning Rick and Pete were waiting for him at the front gate, squatting on the ground by the logging camp gate sign. Still drunk from the previous night's debauch, they could hardly talk, let alone sensibly. They spoke to one another in Navajo in a tone that sounded caustic, then they walked up to Frank's truck where Pete pulled out a .22 caliber pistol and held it in his hand. He didn't aim it at Frank, but handed it to him, barrel down, with a look of terrible resignation.

Frank said, "I can tell you've been drinking, and where did you get that .22 pistol? You know you're not supposed to have any firearms out here."

Rick answered, "A white man bought the gun for us a few weeks ago when we were in town. We've been using it to shoot squirrels above camp. Pete's giving it up to you."

"Pete? Why's Pete giving it to me? Why doesn't he just throw it in the creek if he doesn't want it anymore or give it to the camp owner? I'll have to take it from you now anyway because I know you have it. You guys amaze me. You're drunk again. How do you get all the booze? Where's Clarence?"

"Pete shot him," Rick answered.

"Pete shot Clarence? What the hell for? What have you done? You have made an absolute mess of things. My God! You killed that poor kid? Oh, my God! This is trouble now. Where'd you leave his body? Good God! I'll have to get the sheriff out here. You guys are too much. . . They'll probably arrest me this time for contributing to the delinquency of minors. The only delinquency I'm guilty of, though, is not tying and gagging you."

Rick pointed to the trees behind the bunkhouse, just beyond a large deck of branded spruce logs. Frank put the pistol on the pickup seat, then got out of his truck and walked toward the timber with the Indians. When he turned the corner past the bunkhouse he saw Clarence's body lying in the bushes, boot toes pointing north and east. They walked over to the body and stood there for a couple of minutes, Frank trying to decide what steps he needed to take.

As they were looking down at Clarence, however, Frank thought he noticed the body twitch. He said to Rick and Pete, "He's still alive, you fools, isn't he? My God, yes, he's still alive. I think he just likes helicopter rides; but he won't get one today! I'm not going to do that again. Where did you shoot him, Pete? Is it serious? I don't see any blood."

"In the belly," said Pete.

Frank looked at Clarence's belly, but saw no blood. He looked closer. What he saw was a large indentation in Clarence's gold rodeo buckle.

*

Thinking about his eventful summer with the Indian crew, Frank nudged the speedometer up to seventy-five miles per hour. He watched the cattle and fenceposts of the Palouse country fly past. In Colfax he picked up a hitchhiker, another college student on his way to Bellingham. In expensive sunglasses with long blond hair blowing in the prairie wind, the hitchhiker and his traveling companion dog, an oddly shaped Husky, were waiting next to the village A&W Drive-in. Frank took pity on them and let them aboard the Plymouth.

As the three drove out of town up a grade to the north, the passenger rolled down his window and smiled at a farmer. The man had stopped his tractor at a railroad crossing and was waiting patiently for the train to pass. The hitchhiker's dog placed its paws on the top of the front seat and pushed its nose into the hitchhiker's ear.

As Frank cornered sharply out of the grade, the passenger's car door flew wide open and he screamed, "What the hell is going on? What's with your damned door?" Grabbing at the dash to keep from falling out the doorway he said, "If I'd been leaning on that thing I'd be dead now."

"I'm sorry. I really am sorry I didn't warn you about that," offered Frank. "Sometimes it flies open. I usually use a clothes hanger to keep it shut. Here." He reached into the back seat and grabbed a wire, then handed it to his rider.

Looking down at the floor in front of his seat the passenger saw a five-inch diameter hole and the highway asphalt speeding beneath it. He had accidentally pushed a wire floor mat out of place. Noticing this, Frank said, "Don't worry. Rocks only come up through that hole on dirt roads."

"So you're guaranteeing that my foot won't suddenly poke through the bottom here? Are you sure? It looks kind of corroded around the edges."

"Just don't put any pressure around the border of the hole," Frank cautioned, pointing. "It's kind of flaking there. Bad rust. I think the previous owner parked the car in water, maybe saltwater."

"I'm taking my life in my hands riding with you, aren't I?"

"Not really. I'm not used to riders, I guess."

As the passenger wrapped the door handle with the wire, his Husky jumped into the front seat. "She thought I was getting out just now, I suppose," said the rider. "Get in the back seat, Sally!"

"What's wrong with your dog?"

"You mean, why does she look like she ate a medicine ball?"

"Yeah."

"Well, we had an accident before we left Reno. I bought a flea bomb to get rid of her fleas and the ones in my apartment. When I set the thing off I didn't do it right. I had the can turned the wrong way and breathed a large dose. I ran out of the room thinking that Sally was following me, but she wasn't. She breathed a lot of the chemical in the bomb. I drove her to the vet and went to the hospital myself to get a lung treatment. The vet said he didn't know why she had swelled that way, but said it would probably go away. One of my own lungs almost collapsed."

Frank wanted to laugh but didn't. The dog looked pathetic. "So will Sally get better?"

"I hope so," said the passenger. "But the vet made no promises."

Frank stopped the car in Ritzville at a coffeeshop for breakfast. The eatery was sandwiched between a one-room insurance agency and the Post Office. It had a flag at full mast on a pole at the curb. "You'd think they'd fly that thing at half mast all day long, every day, with all the dead bodies piling up in Vietnam," said the passenger. "But no, they have to have a politician die to justify flying the flag at half mast."

"I suppose you're right. I hadn't thought of it that way."

As they walked into the café a woman came out the door. When she saw the passenger she scowled in his direction. Frank knew it was the passenger's long hair and Navy P coat.

The inside of the Oasis Coffeeshop was paneled front to back in dark knotty pine. Between the knotty pine booths was wallpaper with a northwestern flair: trout fishermen in blue water up to the hips with long flyrods and huge rainbow trout leaping in twists, silver lures draped from their mouths. A snow-capped mountain was painted behind each fisherman at every booth, its summit crowned with white mist.

They slid into a booth across from a white and gray marble counter with red plastic stools, a 1930s-style soda fountain and candy counter. The cook in the kitchen was singing 'Love Is Blue' before a farmer at the end of the counter punched in a Merle Haggard number on the jukebox.

The middle-aged waitress walked slowly and peripherally toward their table, then dropped yellowing menus and two glasses of water at the rim of the tabletop. She then disappeared into the kitchen. After she was out of sight, Frank noticed the cook's thin face and brushy eyebrows poke through the service slot to look in their direction.

"I guess we look interesting," Frank said, taking off his corduroy jacket. "I'm hungry for apple pie and cheddar."

"What's this thing on the menu called Washington nut pie?" asked the passenger.

"That's pecan pie. Up here they call it Washington nut."

"Pecans are from Louisiana, I thought," the rider said.

"In this state they come from Yakima."

"So why don't they call it Yakima nut pie? I suppose it doesn't sound patriotic enough. Too Indian."

"A good question, indeed," said Frank, humoring him.

The waitress took their order standing three feet from the table. As she stared at the rider Frank, too, took a closer look at his week-old beard. When Frank squinted, the beard looked like the bandana of a robber. He turned and looked out the window and noticed a Marine recruitment sign in front of the Post Office.

"So you're going to school in Bellingham?" Frank asked.

"Yeah. I finished work a couple of weeks ago."

"Where'd you work for the summer?"

"L.A."

"Doing what?"

"My uncle had connections at a bomb factory. Before that I was working for a guy who made bathtub and sink stoppers. I ran two machines. I must've made one- or two-hundred-thousand plugs. Slave labor. Twelve hours a day. Seven days a week. I got sick of it, so my uncle got me the job making bombs."

"Real bombs? Not bug bombs or something like that one you had in Reno?"

"Yeah, real bombs. The Vietnam kind. The B-52 bomber kind. In Watts. I almost got the hell beat out of me several times by some of the black dudes at that plant, but an old guy there kind of took me under his wing and stood up for me. I was white in a sea of black. So what did *you* do this summer, Mr. Ideeho?"

"Well, I was logging, driving rubber-tire skidder and doing maintenance work at a logging machinery shed. A skidder's a tractor with big wheels that drags logs out of the timber. I also had an Indian crew to watch out for."

The waitress dropped off pie and coffee and kept going toward the other end of the cafe. The passenger began to eat. As he ate he looked up at the fish on the wallpaper. Between bites he observed, "Notice that fish's eye. It kind of looks out at the world, but not at anything in particular. I worked with a guy like that this summer. I suppose there are a lot of people like that, who never quite get focused on what's going on around them.

"So you were a logger?"

"I did that and helped my girlfriend with a science project she started."

"What was that?"

"Some kind of animal counting thing. She got some money from the state to count chukars."

"Really? That's cute."

"Excuse me?"

"Nothing. This pie is pretty damned good. What's a chukar?"

"Some kind of bird, like a wild pigeon. What are you studying up at Bellingham?"

"Chemistry. It's my second year, and philosophy. I was the head of SDS in my high school in California. I've started a chapter at Western Washington." The passenger looked at Frank closely for a reaction.

"You don't mean that radical student group, do you?"

The rider looked at Frank and made a ghoul's face, then groaned huskily, "WOOAA. . . BOOOOO!!!"

"What's the SDS stand for?"

"Soup, donuts, and salvation."

"Come on, really."

"Students for a Democratic Society."

"Sounds okay to me. Who could be against that?"

"You're a naïve fucker, aren't you?"

"What do you mean?"

"It's not the young republicans, knucklehead farmboy."

"So the democratic is a joke?"

"Have you ever heard of Karl Marx?"

"The Communist?"

"No, the Marx brother. Of course, yes, the Communist."

"Oh. They let you have a Communist club at your high school? That's pretty weird. And at college, too?"

"Yeah."

"I'm going to college on an ROTC scholarship."

"Great. So you're going to Vietnam?" The passenger asked the question with contempt.

"I don't know yet. You seem to have done your share of contributing to the war making bombs that can destroy women and children and cats and dogs."

"What I did as a laborer is irrelevant."

"Oh, I see. It's the pilot's fault that the bombs might explode if they accidentally hit a non-military target."

"It's the system's fault. The system has to be changed so people don't have to earn their bread making bombs. We're talking fundamentals. But then, what would you know up here in the outback of old I-dee-hoe?"

"Yeah, we're just a bunch of bo-diddlies. We have to depend on you Californians to bring us words of wisdom from outside the county. You know? You're a real pain in the ass kind of person. I think you can catch another ride to Bellingham pretty easily. How long they'll travel with you, well, that's another question. You might end up freezing to death along the roads of Eastern Washington fending for yourself."

"Thank you," the passenger sneered.

"No problem."

"Want to see my horns?"

"What are you talking about? You play a clarinet, too?"

"They're under my hair. The devil horns grow under my hair, little nubs. Shall I show you?"

"You're nuts."

"I know. I'm a commie, a pinko. We're all nuts, villains. That was clear to the waitress and cook when we walked in here. Why'd it take you so long to notice? You better do something about that naivete of yours, Mr. Frank."

"You know, you're right. I'll get right on it."

"My old man's a colonel in the Air Force. I've had to live with the military garbage all my life. At some point, I got sick of it."

"Your father is an officer in the U.S. Air Force?"

"Yes. And I'm his creepy son, the anti-fascist, anti-imperialist, communist son of revolution who makes his old man puke. Are you going to serve in the U.S. armed forces in Vietnam?"

"That sounds like the question of an officer of the Peoples Republic of North Vietnam. I probably will, yes."

"Then you're a fascist and an imperialist."

"Thanks for the labels. I don't see any reason to discuss this, Mr. Name Caller from California. You wouldn't accept any justification I could give you for going over there. Besides, maybe

I will just have to go over there because I'm forced to, even if I don't want to go."

"That's true. So you *don't* want to go?"

Frank and his passenger reached a dead-end in their conversation and sat there silently. Frank didn't want to discuss his situation with an SDS leader. After all, he figured the passenger's reasons for opposing the war would not parallel his own. When the waitress came by and asked if they wanted more coffee, the rider said, "Sure, we'll take more coffee. We don't want the market to dry up for the South American natives."

The waitress looked perplexed and walked off after pouring the coffee.

"Look," said Frank. "Why don't you tell me about your father? Tell me something about the man I'm going to meet. I have a new commander to report to at my detachment in Seattle. I'd like to learn something. We can at least learn something from one another?"

"Ah, yes, sure, indeedy we can," said the passenger. "Back to less important things."

"So tell me what it was like being the Communist son of a U.S. Air Force colonel."

The rider leaned back in the booth and took a cigarette out of his chest pocket. "So you want to know about my father, the colonel? How about if I begin with my grandfather? He was a Russian aristocrat before the revolution. After fleeing to America he got a job in Washington, D.C., some unimportant position in an agency that handled finances, the U.S. Treasury or Office of Management and Budget, something like it I recall. He told my father when he was growing up that he'd been in the Russian army at one time and told him stories of battles he'd been in. My old man then proved his own valor in WW II. But you can't keep a line of militarism going on in a family forever. Someone always breaks the daisy chain. That's where I come in. What better way to demonstrate Hegel's dialectic than my being a Communist, don't you think? The synthesis at the end of several generations of warmongers?" The passenger chuckled.

Frank took a drink of coffee. The passenger continued chuckling, out of control, as if he'd been smoking grass or hashish. Frank could tell the conversation was over for the time being. He looked at the tab, left several dollars and a tip, and went out to the car. There he waited with Sally until the passenger came out the door of the café.

The next day he wrote this dream in his journal:

— At a large military base I was racing around meeting different people, introducing myself, learning names, talking fast, bowing and laughing. Everyone was having a drink and spilling it on the person standing or sitting next to them.

*

A week later in Seattle Frank met his new commander. There had been a change of the guard since he started the program a year earlier. The previous commander had shipped out for Florida.

"Cadet, this is Captain Dugan." Lieutenant Swenson introduced the football player of a man in Navy whites. The commander turned away from his substantial wife who was wearing a rosy Hawaiian gown. He looked at Frank.

"This is Cadet Ravan, Sir," said Swenson.

"Sir," said Frank, now at attention.

"At ease, Cadet," the commander said, reaching to shake Frank's hand. "This is Louise, my wife. Everything is informal tonight. It's a night for introductions. Some of the girls from the Navy support society are here, too. I'm sure you'll want to meet them. Tuesday morning at drill will be soon enough for salutes."

Frank nodded to the commander and his wife, self-conscious of his ill-fitting uniform and unshined shoes.

"That's a most elegant dress, Louise," said the lieutenant.

"Why thank you, Bob. I got it in Hawaii, of course."

Frank said, "Yes, that is a lovely dress." After he said it he blushed red and the lieutenant and commander smiled at him.

"Well, thank you, Cadet. I like this potential officer, Bob," Captain Dugan's wife said.

The commander looked amused. He said, "Cadet, could you please get my wife another drink?"

"Certainly, Sir. My pleasure, Sir." In a moment he was on the way to the bar on behalf of the commander, to fill his wife's wineglass. He thought of the couple as he approached the bar. She had a silver bird on a silver chain around her neck. He had very tired eyes, deeply sunken, and thick salt and pepper eyebrows. The strain of decision-making was apparent in the commander's face. His wife appeared comfortable being the wife of the man at the helm.

"Tell me, Cadet," the commander said after Frank returned with the drink, "What is your major?"

"I still haven't declared one, Sir. I want to study literature, among other subjects."

"Well, most of our cadets are in engineering and the sciences. Remember, there's not much use for philosophy and literature in the military. History, well, that's a good background. Enjoy the food." The commander, with his wife on his wing, pivoted toward the buffet, leaving Frank with the lieutenant.

The lieutenant then delivered his 'lecture to the humanities majors.' "Literature is frowned upon in the military, Frank. You already know that. If you think you might go in that direction you'll have an uphill climb on promotions. The military is run by science and engineering types. We don't mean to discourage your interests. Just remember that there's a lot going on in philosophy and the arts and literature today that should be entirely disregarded. Horace and other ancients writing about war are one thing, but literature for literature's sake, well, that won't get you anywhere.

"That English chap, Bertrand Russell, is causing a lot of trouble at the universities. He's on campus this month, in fact. Even in mathematics circles young people are losing their sense of purpose. We in the military pay the tab for people like him who don't respect nationalism and moral integrity. Subversion of good values is popular on campuses all across America right now. It's really sad that we pay such a price for democracy. I don't mean to indicate that all philosophy is suspect. In fact, a little oriental philosophy is also good for the soul now and then.

"An orderly I had at Da Nang, a fellow who did my gardening, a young gook, well actually a Chinese, now he was a master philosopher. He always said something witty or helpful. He used to take care of my garden, as I said. I used to dig around out there with him once in a while. He'd turn to me while trimming weeds and say things like: 'Through compassion one triumphs in attack and is impregnable in defense.' Then we'd have a good laugh. He was a good person, good for my spirit anyway. He read a lot. Yes, sir, that gook knew his philosophy. 'The gateway of the mysterious female is the root of heaven and earth.' Is that Chinese? It just came back to me."

"Yes, Sir. It sounds Chinese."

"By the way, Ravan. You're not a married cadet, are you?"

"No, Sir. I'm in a dormitory. Fleishing."

"Oh, yes, the high-rise. You'll need to find some other cadets in the building. You need to hang together. The atmosphere on campus has turned very negative this year; probably a lot to do with that Woodstock dope-smoking concert and the Manson murders. Hang with other corpsmen and you'll feel less isolated. Find another cadet to room with if you can. I can help you if you like."

HUNTERS

The forest was irregularly shadow-filled or black this time of morning as the pickup truck tilted over hi-bars, headlights shooting unwieldy arcs of light up the mountain road, illuminating banks of withered beargrass blooms and green-brown undergrowth. On the west side of the mountain morning came slowly, sunlight filtering through steep spruce-covered foliage. Coming out of a little bog the headlights caught a cow elk standing in the middle of the road. Her eyes gleamed in the headlights.

"Look at her!" Don said as he hit the brakes.

He and Frank jumped from the pickup with their rifles and leaned ribcages against the front hood of the truck. Just as they raised their rifle barrels, however, the elk's umber flanks launched her into a gallop and she sailed over a 45-degree drop past the road's edge, crashing into timber and underbrush. Neither Frank nor Don could get a shot off. She was over the road's dusty lip before they could even find their safety buttons.

The noise woke Brid, who had been asleep in the cab of the truck. "You know how to get my attention, don't you!" she scolded Frank.

"It's time you got up, don't you think?" He gave Brid a kiss and reached for a thermos of coffee.

Don had walked to the point where the cow had disappeared. Back now he informed them, "She's loooong gone."

"I thought you couldn't shoot cows," said Brid.

"Not the case this year," Don noted. "The herd's so large they opened it up for both bulls and cows."

"Are you going to follow her for a while?" Brid asked Frank.

"Yeah. We'll go a few miles. It'll be light soon."

"When the sun comes up I'll go up into those rocks and read. I brought my book, binoculars, and tea. I'll wait for you there. If it gets any colder I'll meet you back at the truck. It's supposed to snow this afternoon, you know. Don't you boys stray too far."

"We'll need clouds to get a storm and I don't see a single one," said Don.

"I don't think the weather will get too foul," Frank agreed.

Don laced up a boot, put a candy bar in his pocket and a pinch of chewing tobacco in his cheek. "Want a bite?" he asked Frank.

"You know what I think of that crud!" Frank said. "You can hand me a cigar though."

"Fresh out," said Don.

"See you fellows later," said Brid, already breaking for the hill.

Don watched her walk away and Frank noticed Don's watching. Before his conversation with Don as he was leaving Welder's Lake heading for Seattle he hadn't noticed the attention Don seemed to give her. Now he stared at him. Don sensed the look and turned away, pretending not to notice Frank, who said simply, "I'll go high. You chase them up to me. I'll meet you at the upper end of the canyon wall on the creek. We can come back together from there. Sound about right?"

"Fine with me," said Don, unzipping his jacket mechanically.

"I'm leaving now, then," said Frank, striding off. He avoided thinking further about the mild interest he'd just seen Don show Brid. He walked to the southwest for several miles, then rested for a half hour before climbing up and along the ridge. At the top of the ridge nearly two hours later he saw a long thread of white across the sky to the north. A red fox raced out of a thicket of alders on the left and along the ridgetop. In the distance a trio of deer bounded out of sight, at least three or four hundred yards away. Now they were headed down over the slope toward where Don was supposed to be coming up to meet Frank.

Frank had come home, in part, to attend Tom Petrella's funeral. He had not been close to Tom in high school as Tom had made decisions to stay in the valley for life and not go to college, and he hung with a crowd that Frank had little in common with. While inseparable as boys, they had gone very different directions as teens. The funeral had reminded him of Jimmy Samsin's; no one had expected it so there was a stunned sensation common among attendees. By now Frank was also used to people dying violently in a mountain and river community where normal precautions never seemed enough to prevent tragedy. Someone always stepped over a line and was instantly killed.

He walked, noticing flagstones of gray-white rock on the ground and short granite blocks pushing up above clumps of grass. Several of them were perfect tombstones. He sat on one of them and ate a candy bar, then an orange, scattering the peel over the ground. Surrounding him were patches of still brown and reddish-green timothy that gave off a silver sheen when the wind blew. He brushed an insect off his neck and recalled the dream he'd had the night before last.

— I was on a rock beside a lake with two women. One woman had dark brown eyes and looked at me. The other woman was looking away and I could not see her eyes. It was September in the dream, very cool, with strong wind making waves on the cold surface of the lake.

Frank got up and walked toward the upper end of the canyon below the ridge. He made his way through deadwood, past anthills and hundreds of stumps in an old clear-cut and just before winding back to the truck he heard a shot. He waited for a second shot, but heard none. He picked up his pace heading back to Brid and Don.

In about twenty minutes he caught sight of Don kneeling over a deer that he had apparently shot. Coming up to him, Frank could see that he was finishing up gutting the carcass. There was blood all over Don's thighs and hands. His buck knife was gritty and stuck in a log.

Neither of them said a word to the other, recognizing the killing event as a moment of metaphysical caution or consideration. Most other hunters they knew were loud and celebratory over their kills, but, in particular, the incident with the deer slaughter at the notch going back to Sea and Frankie's childhood and involving Brid's O'Seetley relatives had set a different tone for the Ravan boys, a quiet respect at any unglulate's death. In a pact the brothers had vowed to handle respectfully the large game they killed to feed their family. This sense always accompanied their rituals after shooting game, and Don was no different, having become familiar with and agreeing with these views. He, too, treated deer and elk with a certain reverence, going so far as to speak thanks to them during butchering.

It was just a few minutes before Don had the deer over his shoulder and Frank was carrying their rifles. A plastic bag with the deer's heart and liver hung from Don's belt. Frank tied red bandanas around the deer's hooves, then the two hunters sidled along the mountain toward a trail that would lead them back up to the road.

At the trailhead they stopped and slung the deer from a thin pole to make carrying it easier, evenly distributing the weight of the deer. They paused momentarily and drank from a nearby spring

where water collected deep and cold in pyrite-speckled pools, then
continued marching along the trail to meet Brid.

*

At the road's intersection with the trailhead Frank walked up
the hill to get Brid while Don waited below with the deer, caught
his breath and took a drink of canteen water.

Nearing Brid Frank yelled, "Ready to go home?"

"I heard a shot," she said.

"Don got his deer."

"I could never kill a deer."

"I know you couldn't."

"I mean a big animal like that. It would make me too sad."

"So, did you see any of those chukars you were looking for?"

"The grouse?"

"Yeah. I mean grouse. I guess it's been a while since you did
the chukar thing."

"There were some. I saw three. This area has a large
population. Frank, when will I see you after this week, after you
take me back to Lewiston?"

"Well, I'll be back through Lewiston at the end of next month. I could swing by your rooming house and bring you back with me to the Notch."

"I'll already be home by then. My break always comes a week before yours. You know I'm really not sure about going away this winter. You'll grow unhappy with me if I'm not around. You'll find someone new after I'm away for just a little while. Then I won't be good enough for you, no matter how hard I try to be."

"Where are you getting this idea? You're not projecting your own tendencies on me, are you?"

"It's just true. No psychology, honest. You could have a lot of girls if you wanted them. Lots of them already like you. I see how they look at you."

"What about you? Even Don would take you away from me if he could manage your uncertainties. I can see it in his eyes sometimes."

"I promise I'll be better, Frank. Just don't leave me because I'm going away for a while. I'm really good for you, and I'll be better."

"Look, where's this rush about being 'better' coming from? You're fine. What have you been thinking about up here all by yourself? You're making me feel uncomfortable. You're the only woman I want, the only one I care about. I love all your ways. I know you. I trust you. I'm always anxious to see you, always. A couple of times I've thought about other girls, even had a tiny wandering crush, but it's never lasted, never, and it's never felt like anything more than a weird moment.

"Whenever we've been apart, I've written you every two or three days now for how long? You're the one I'm worried about. If you only knew the guys who've been waiting for us to split up so they could step into my place. I've realized that sometimes you seem so lonely, even when I'm around. I don't know why. I begin to think you'll get so lonely you'll just start another relationship. Maybe I can't talk with you about the things you really need or something like that. Is that true? If you had more friends I wouldn't worry so much."

"All I need is you, Frank. I'll be better. When I come back I'll make you the happiest man alive."

Frank was confused why their conversation had headed in this direction. He thought how beautiful Brid was with her hair pinned up in the back and that faint feline smile at the corner of her lips, a smile that, nevertheless, made him doubt in some ways that he really did know her. She didn't always smile at him in the same way.

"I have enough friends, Frank. But you have so many friends that I sometimes feel dispensable. You're friendly with everyone you know, and you seem to know everyone. You find out about people quickly and they warm up to you. How can you need me when you have so many friends and want to do so many things all the time? It seems that new experiences are all you want out of life. Long ago I should have suggested we settle down here in Idaho and take over a home place somewhere."

As Brid touched Frank's arm she saw the restlessness in his green eyes that over the years had almost grown more gray than green. The wind blew his collar up. And even when she saw this restlessness she sensed his peace about it. He was going to have a life of peace no matter what went on around him. There was a bedrock somewhere under there and Frank seemed to have his feet on it.

Brid folded her arms as Frank took them and looked into her eyes. Sometimes when he looked into her she would turn away, a sign he took as shyness. As she turned away to look out over the canyon he could no longer see as much color in her irises. It seemed to lighten, affected somehow by the grays of the sky and greens of the forest.

"There's a lot we both want to do, Brid. I don't want to stand in your way. I love you. And even if I have to be a long way away for a while, we'll get back together eventually, once and for all. If you want to be with me why don't you come to school in Seattle?"

"Why don't you come to school with me in Lewiston?" she asked.

"Well, that defines our problem and our challenge. There's not much left to say when we get to this point every time we talk about it. It'll work out, Brid. You have to do what you need to, and so do I. That must be right."

"I want it to work out, Frank. I really do. We'll both have to be strong for each other."

"Yes, we will."

"We'll both have to try our best."

"Yes, we will."

Frank sat back against a rock and looked past the Indian paintbrush and skunk cabbage to the canyon below. Brid leaned against his chest and he put his arm around her shoulder. Her blowing hair tickled his face and he brushed it back with his fingers several times.

*

The next evening Frank headed back to Seattle. He left Brid in Lewiston. It had snowed a half-inch cover on the desert of Eastern Washington. There were a few deer and antelope running along the highway, and slain deer strapped to the sides or tops of cars and trucks that passed along the highway. Clean-shaven and stubble-faced hunters alike filled the cafes where Frank stopped for coffee and pie. Late that evening, in the midst of another light snowstorm Frank pulled into a twenty-four-hour truckstop called The Whitetail.

Hunters lined the counters wearing florescent-colored vests and hats and the waitresses were working overtime. Above the tables on all the walls were deer, elk and moose antlers and Charles Russell prints. At the cash register was a basket full of little pins with a picture of a mounted whitetail deer.

That night in Seattle Frank dreamed of shooting a deer. The next day he wrote in his journal:

— *Panting hard after racing up a small hill, I leaned against a lodgepole tree trunk. I raised the rifle, aimed high and slowly pulled the trigger. The deer's gray-brown body fell instantly with the blast of the casing. I stared in disbelief for a moment, then ran straight up the hill a hundred more feet to the deer, my legs feeling heavy. The guttural wail of the animal dying gave me chills. I had broken its spine, leaving it to flounder down the slope until it became entrapped beneath a partially fallen log. I raised the rifle again and aimed at the animal's throat. The ensuing blast tore a hole in its neck, letting a river of hot mauve blood gurgle out. I fell to my knees at the awfulness of the event. The creature began to grow in size in the dream. It grew as big as an Egyptian statue. Beyond the slain deer I saw two confused fawns bound through thick buckbrush. There was nothing left to do. I called to the fawns but they kept leaping through the brush until they disappeared.*

Sickness unto Death

Frank answered the dorm room door. He had just put his running shoes and clean socks in a basket by the door. His roommate Alan was reading Kierkegaard and sitting with legs akimbo on his bunk.

Bursky was at the door in bellbottom jeans, pullover black sweater and sneakers. He had a doggerel, clean-shaven expression framed in long burnt orange hair and sideburns, a perpetually guilty look about him. He was one of a few Vietnam veterans Frank had met and spoken with during his first two years of college.

"How's the Nav-Rot-C guy?" he asked Frank.

"Just fine," Frank said. "Hey Alan, your girlfriend's here to see you."

"Very funny, Navy fly guy," said Bursky.

"Come on in, Bursk," Alan said.

Frank sat down on his bunk. He was trying to fix an alarm clock that had been knocked on the floor and broken.

"You know, Frank. You ought to talk to Bursky more about the war. He knows a helluva lot more than we do about what's really going on over there."

Frank had been cold to Bursky after meeting him. He seemed crude and sneaky, even a bit deranged. Alan and he smoked dope together. Being civil, he said to Bursky, "Are you on the GI bill?"

"You got it. Back from Nam now three months. Never been happier."

"Marines, right?"

"Leathernecks, indeed!"

"How long were you there?"

"Long enough to know I wanted to get the first plane out. If the gooks don't get you, heroin will. If the *horse* don't get you, the *horz* will. I had eighteen months. Didn't want any more."

Alan closed his book and joined the conversation. "Bursky's in my sociology class. We're doing a paper together. I asked him to come by and talk about the war. Do you care, Frank, if we light a J?"

"No, just crack the window. I've got to report to the gym in an hour. Maybe you saw more than your share of drugs and prostitution, Bursky."

"There was a lot more to it, sure. But it's a wrongheaded shithole. There's no reason for us to be over there. We're just screwing up those people worse than they're already screwed up. There are whole canvas cities the size of Puyallup full of Vietnamese prostitutes. Worse yet, the prostitute ops are handled by the U.S. Government.

"And dope is their daily bread. Anything you want, on base or off. After you've been on a few killing missions, the dope is pretty gooood. You neeeed it. It keeps your mind off what's reeeelly goin' on. Blue morphine. That's heaven on earth. Cheap heaven. I did it twice but didn't dare do it again.

"Grass. That was my thing. I brought a lot back with me. I'll bring some over some night. It's stronger than these garden clippings you guys get from Oatville." Bursky held up the joint he was smoking with Alan.

Frank was hearing things he'd never heard before and he didn't want to hear them, but he couldn't pull himself away from the conversation. "Don't you think the Vietnamese want their country back?" asked Frank.

"Who has it? You mean, want it back from us? There are no Vietnamese and Vietcong. There are only Vietnamese. The ones in the north we just call Vietcong, they are also Vietnamese. And the ones in the south we call Vietnamese, they're Vietcong. They're all one people. *We're* the enemy in Vietnam, not the Cong. That's what makes the war so crazy."

Frank asked, "So you think we Americans are imposing our way of life on Vietnam and if we aren't there anymore everything will be okay? The Jane Fonda viewpoint?"

Bursky took another hit, then exhaled slowly. "Is there any other way to view what's going on there? South Vietnam is not a democracy. It's a puppet government, a puppet government of Western powers. Ho Chi Minh tried for years to get Americans to help him get French colonials out of his country and we refused.

Good old Harry True Man wouldn't help him; neither would Ike, or JFK, or LBJ. Now we've got Tricky Dick dropping bombs on Vietnam, Cambodia, *and* Laos. I don't think what's going on in Vietnam has anything to do with civil war."

"That's a pretty pat opinion. As a soldier, how would you have the whole perspective on what we should or shouldn't be doing there?"

"Look, Frank, you seem like a good guy. You want to do your part. So did I. In fact, I did my part, and it was like climbing into a nightmare machine."

"War is a nightmare. I'm not sure I want to do my part in this particular war."

"No, Frank. You don't know what a nightmare is. I think in some wars men can hang onto some code that keeps them going despite what they see or experience. Vietnam's not the same thing. It can't be. I don't want to know what I know."

"Every war has stuff you can't bear to think about."

"Well, Frank. Could you please take my memories and give me a new brain? I'll give you everything I own in exchange, and that includes a thousand-acre cattle ranch I stand to inherit in Oregon. I never asked to see Vietnamese women and children killed. I had buddies who took bets on how far their Vietcong prisoners could run after they released them before they were shot. There were bets on everything. We placed bets on whether or not you could shoot a guy's leg or arm off with one M-16 round, and from how far away, or whether. . . God, I can't even tell you the other shit some of the GIs used to do. . . My God!"

"You're a sick man, Bursky," Frank said. "You should have reported this stuff."

"Reported it to the perps? Yes, I'm a sick man here in Washington state, but I was normal in Vietnam, Frank. You have no idea."

Frank was nauseous and pale. He was hearing more and more of this kind of talk from Bursky and soon there would be others to corroborate some of it. Bursky should be arrested, he thought, and all the other men like him. How could his country sanction this kind of thing?

"They're going to run us out of their country in a few years. We'll win dogshit over there; that's all. We're intruders in Vietnam, no matter how good some of our intentions are."

"You mean we don't adhere to the Geneva accords on prisoners of war?" Frank asked.

"Frank! Get real, man. Take a hit," said Bursky, laughing sardonically. "You need a smoke. You're in fantasyland. Have a hit of grass; that's the only reality I've come to know."

"You should have reported this stuff if it was criminal."

"Frank, you do a great broken record. The common practice in our patrols was to kill prisoners of war before returning to base. I shot plenty of them on direct orders. The guys in my platoon used to make a game of it. I saw prisoners shot to death slowly, limb by limb. I saw them shot in the back when they were told to run for their lives. I saw them naked and sprayed with bullets, ripped in half, you name it. One time a chopper picked up our prisoners and took care of them for us. We watched them all pushed out the chopper doorways several hundred feet above the jungle horizon, taking bets the whole time about how many 180-degree flips the bodies would make before they hit the paddy.

"There's no humanity in war. There's no civilized war. There's only talk about civilized war in classrooms, seminars and at war vet luncheons. The fact is that you can't afford to take prisoners many times. And only soldiers know that. Civilians think they can have rules for war. Civilians can't conceive of war unless it's boxed by Milton Bradley. There's no law and no humanity in war.

"I accepted that; then I went over to the jungles and shot my share of gooks."

"Gooks?" asked Alan.

"Yeah, gooks," said Bursky resignedly. "That's how you start to think of them. I know it's not a popular term in sociology classes. Look, when I went over there, instead of burning my draft card or splitting the country, I knew what those people would be like. Like me, right? NO! I couldn't *let* them be. They had to be just plain gooks for me to do what I did."

Alan was embarrassed. He thought of himself as a radical and here was a friend of his making him look bad by being politically incorrect: calling the Vietnamese gooks.

"Look," said Bursky, "Maybe you guys don't want to hear about Vietnam at all. Hey, just crawl into your little warm cocoons. Have Mommy and Daddy send you your checks. Stay in a dormitory. Get some rosy pussy from Bellevue. Smoke a little weed. Vietnam will be over soon anyway. Look, there are too many coffins showing up on the evening news! How long do you think 'the silent majority' can stand that?"

"If you guys think we should invade another country I've got a good opportunity for you. One of my Marine buds was delivered to Vietnam on a transport that came through the Middle East. It stopped at a place called Yemen. He and another GI got off the boat for a short leave and they saw a poster that said there was going to be a *stoning* that afternoon. They were curious so they wound their way across the port city to the sight where this thing was supposed to happen. At the magic hour they brought a woman down to a little plaza and tied her to a post, then a god-damned dumptruck backed up to her and emptied a load of boulders on top of her. Now that's sick! Apparently, this is common in places like that; it's their version of modernity. So why don't we invade Yemen and impose a little democracy there? In Vietnam, we're too often the ones backing up those trucks full of rock!"

Frank was feeling a little high from second-hand smoke. He looked into Bursky's face, at the cigarette he'd just lit in the corner of his mouth. The smoke curled into vipers around his head, then obscured the Swiss Alps ski poster on the wall. Bursky was in uniform, standing at the edge of a rice paddy. His cigarette was a joint. A rifle was slung over his shoulder. His helmet was tipped up. Dull green grenade bulbs were wrapped in wadding across his chest. Three prisoners in black uniforms cowered on the ground.

"Let's get back to base," said Bursky.

"How do you want to waste them? Who's turn is it?" asked one soldier.

"You mean who gets to cheat it this time?" asked another.

"Yeah. It's Bursky's turn. Do it Bursky."

*

Frank's feet hit the last landing in the fire escape before he could get control of the images swirling in his head. Bursky had been to visit Alan for the umpteenth time. Frank had heard stories from other GIs about their Vietnam experiences, but Bursky's were the worst and perhaps most real in terms of what they might reveal. They had the kind of detail that made you sense some kind of underlying truth. They could have represented overstatement, but Bursky had no real stake in telling wild tales or shocking people; at least Frank could see none.

He was considering giving up his scholarship. There was total chaos in the press about what was happening in Vietnam. Why are Americans there? Who is the enemy? Who is right? Anybody? Conscience? Reason? The U.S. Navy? The Pentagon? State Department? Oval Office? American Legion? American history?

Frank weighed the pacifist option. To be consistent with it he would always have to evaluate constantly how his personal ethics compared to everything the state stood for. He would have to profess the irrational: it is improper to kill any life, even to destroy a wicked enemy such as Hitler or the Nazi state. Under a purely pacifist argument, he could not object only to a specific war. He must object to 'all' wars. Frank wanted consistency, but he couldn't go along with this much consistency, and trying to might be an impossible intellectual burden containing the seeds of madness. How could one really evaluate individual action relative to a complex web of dependencies between individuals, society, commerce, and a democratic state?

He didn't believe in the Vietnam War any longer, but he had trouble with the idea of a total exit from the country. What would happen to those in South Vietnam who had been misled over the years into thinking that their country could adapt to an American way of life and government? Wouldn't these people just be massacred when the Americans left the war zone?

An exit from the war therefore must not be too hasty. Frank recalled a conversation he had had with a South Vietnamese lecturer after a symposium at the college. The man, born near Hanoi, had served as an officer for four years in the South Vietnamese army before leaving and traveling abroad to talk to academic communities about the war. He had said to Frank imploringly, "America must reach a peaceful settlement with

North Vietnam and only agree to a gradual, carefully planned exit. America owes this to the good people in the south who are seeking a positive result for their country. Communism *is* a terrible thing, and it may take my people many years to learn how terrible it can be. Unfortunately, the awfulness of Communism has almost lost its meaning in a war zone that has been thoroughly corrupted."

The last question then, was whether Frank ought to continue to support the current— imagining it to be short-term— American military presence in Vietnam. The problem with this view was that he had no control over whether America stayed short-, medium-, or long-term. There was a tide and the tide was now in while America was committed to winning the war, but it was going out fast and he knew the speed would pick up. The war machine would soon be stranded neck-deep in mud.

Becoming a pilot in the military would mean joining something over which Frank had no control. He would be required to participate in acts of violence he could not sanction. Gradually, he might just see the whole war come crashing to a violent finish with his country leaving the south vulnerable and subject to mutilation and humiliation.

He wrote a letter to his congressmen suggesting that America should exit Vietnam, but slowly. He got letters back that were exemplary of the dilemma in the politicians' minds. They said that one was either *for* the war, or *against* it. If you are for it, we stay. If you are against it, we are out of there pronto. He knew it was growing impossible to argue for a diminishing cessation of hostilities. It was increasingly likely that the war would end abruptly and that America would not be able to control how it would end.

*

That winter in Seattle there was more rain than usual, and only one night of snow. Frank became a friend to fog, a perfect brooding companion. He took walks late at night trying to work out the details of his future, passing from one fogbank to another along pastel-lit waterfronts and residential areas near the university district.

He haunted the paths of a lonely park ravine at night where the fog was so thick that after months of wandering there he could still not master the pathways. When he wandered off into ivy, rhododendrons, or roses, he sometimes muddied his feet so thoroughly that he had to leave his shoes outside his dormitory room door before coming in at night.

He once pierced the cornea of his eye so deeply with a thorn from a rose bush that the ROTC program required a special eye examination to ensure that his vision was still good enough to pass a rigorous flight physical. Returning to his room after night walks, his down parka was always soaked through with moisture from the fog or drizzle. It was never quite dry enough to wear the next day even after twelve hours of drying on the back of his desk chair.

It had been a week since Don's father had died. Don called the day it happened, then wrote Frank a letter. One evening while walking, Frank opened the letter and read it. He then read it again and again. Then he took out the last letter he had received from Brid before she left for Spain and read it again. The letters had each gathered so much moisture that the words were getting fuzzy. He tried to dry them two or three times and placed them back inside his parka pocket to prevent further damage.

Dear Frank,

The snow's deep this year. I still can't get used to Dad being gone. His health was improving just before the end, so it was sudden and unexpected when he died. Mom will likely pass away soon, too. She's so full of grief.

I've been to a recruiter. As I told you before, I decided not to enlist because I think my number's coming up anyway. It's kind of a Chinese stick game. The length of duty doesn't matter to me anymore. I'm an American. I'll serve.

We'll have a memorial service for Dad when the snow eases up. Some of the high country folks won't be able to get into the Nook for another month or two. We put Dad in the ground yesterday, a small funeral. O'Seetley's nephew Oltman took the body to the graveyard with his sled and dray horses. It was tough lowering him into that cold dirt. Harry Tower broke a tooth on his old broken-down backhoe digging up the icy ground with the schist in it. I don't know how they found somebody willing to dig up that ground this time of year. I guess there's always a drunk somewhere hard up for a bottle of gin. I think Harry and a friend did all the digging. I'm grateful to them. I'd have done it myself if necessary.

Brid came to the funeral. We went skating on the river ponds afterwards, before she went back to school. She leaves for Spain in a day or two, as you know. She misses you.

Next letter you get from me may be from Vietnam. At least soon I won't have to wonder anymore about the draft. Keep your spirits up, and get out of the service if you can. I'll be contributing enough for two of us.

Your friend,
Don

Frank put the letter away and noticed one of his feet was especially cold. He unlaced the boot, bent his leg and cupped the damp wool sock in his hands. He felt where his one toe was missing and remembered the day he had lost it in the woods with Percy. His grandfather had warned him about standing on ice while splitting firewood. Ignoring the advice, he slipped while swinging the ax and chopped off one of the toes of his left foot. The stub itched terribly sometimes and whenever it did he rubbed or scratched it vigorously. The missing fourth toe had never seemed to impede his running ability unless he was exhausted. He pulled out the second letter.

Dear Frank,

It's very lonely today and I leave tomorrow. I've missed you. Last night I sat on the snowy rock above the stream where we always watch the fish. There's a lot of snow. I sometimes have second thoughts about going this winter, but Don said he was sure you wanted me to go. You'll write me, won't you? I've enclosed a list of addresses and written how long I'll be at each place and how much time you'll have to get letters there before they'll miss reaching me. I will be at the main camp for five weeks toward the end of the tour. If you think your letters might be late, just write to me there.

There's so much on my mind with getting ready to go. I feel like preparation has taken years: the passport, the shots, the camera film, the right books on special order, collecting enough money, getting traveler's checks. I've had to say my share of goodbyes, too, over the past two weeks. Everyone wishes me well.

Don says hello. He's been in a funk since his father died, but we've talked a lot and I think he'll get into better spirits in time. I hope he doesn't get drafted. I'll be afraid every minute he is gone. It's so terrible over there. Lots of soldiers get killed just before they're supposed to ship home. My uncle used to tell me stories about WW II. They were so gruesome. I have a hard time seeing Don as a soldier. He still reads that I Ching *book.*

It will be such a long time to be away from you, and so far away. I still think you'll forget about me one of these days, that you'll find someone better, someone who'll understand you better, someone more intellectual you can talk to. I miss you. Please write.

The geese are all gone now. Funny how some of them like to stay so long into the winter, just waiting around for the water to freeze, it seems. I think it's because of the grain the ranchers leave along the river for the elk. I see lots of geese there with the elk.

There's still a contest in Weldler's Lake about when the lake will freeze. I entered with a date two weeks earlier than Don. If *you send me a date I'll enter it for you. The prize this year is $100. I could enter you in the 'When It Melts' contest, too, if you'd like.*

I think of you always and miss you. I await another letter before I leave tomorrow. I'll be at the Post Office bright and early to check. Keep taking care of yourself.

I love you,
Brid

Frank folded the letter and put it away, thinking that he had not really told Brid much about his views about war or about the fantasies he was having about other women. Don had dampened his desire and willingness to talk with Brid about Vietnam because of the comments he had made about Frank's excessive seriousness. He was feeling distance from Brid because of this.

Frank had also once had a conversation with Don about women he might date if he and Brid were no longer involved. He regretted having shared the information even with a friend because it might still come back at him somehow, even innocently. He remembered Don saying he favored meeting girls with an air of rectitude, but no inhibitions. Frank recalled the event that had so impressed Don. A Mormon girl had pounced him once after a high school dance and his head was spinning with sexual recollections for weeks.

After talking with Don eagerly about several girls he had met and would like to go out with, Frank realized he had said too much. He then pretended that he was exaggerating and really only had eyes for intelligent, dark Irish beauties with long legs like Brid. She was all he wanted. By then, it did not fool Don.

*

It was a cold Saturday morning in January. The fieldhouse was nearly empty except for several baseball players doing batting practice in a huge net cage. Frank could see his breath as he warmed up along a wall, loosening his muscles. His bones were cold, too, and his face muscles were numb with cold. The towel around his neck finally felt warm as he rocked shoulders back and forth over knees and stretched his legs. Every time a batter cracked the baseball the emptiness of the building became apparent, echoing from one end of the vault to the other and sending a pigeon or two scattering through the rafters. Frank laced his running shoes tight and loosened the ankles of his sweat pants.

After kneading his calves one last time, he began to run. The gray walls and high windows grew into two bands that held him on course. The heat flowed across his shoulders after the first ten laps. He pitched the towel off to the side and adjusted his mind to his usual meditation, watching the lines pass under him and the gray wall color surround him. He pumped the cold air into his chest and quickly exhaled thin ribbons of carbon dioxide out the corners of his mouth. His arms worked hard as he struggled to regulate the pace by the clock on the wall above the fieldhouse's drafty front doors.

At the fifteenth 440-yard lap he settled into a fine-tuned, steady pace, increasing his speed about a second every lap up to the thirty lap mark. In the first thirty he concentrated on rhythm. At lap thirty-one he began struggling. His pace became uneven, affected by the pain in his lungs and legs. The air was still so cold. His pace fell eight seconds in the thirty-first lap, so he focused on muscle control, not letting his ankles weaken on the corners. His breathing was now loud and his time more erratic.

After lap forty-five he slowed appreciably and took two laps gliding. Now his missing toe was bothering him. It felt numb along the front of his left foot. He jogged slower until he was just walking fast. He felt as if he was dragging a club foot.

"In comes the good; out goes the bad," he said to himself, dazed. "I'll have to keep this up until spring to be any good at all in the first few track meets." He was now gasping, trying to maintain a flow of air in and out. He walked steadily for a whole lap, then went over and grabbed a towel to wrap around his neck. He headed for the showers.

After fully cooling down and standing in the showers he realized that Brid was now already gone, on her way to the other side of the globe. Don would be headed for Vietnam soon, based on his latest expectations.

Weak from running, Frank felt powerless. The blood in his body flowed to his feet, making him lightheaded. He fell against the tile wall of the showers, then slid down. He did not pass out, but his vision momentarily went dark. A baseball player who'd come into the clubhouse said to him through the showers doorway, "Are you okay, Jock?"

Frank muttered "Yes" and got to his feet. A few locker doors slammed and a wooden bench was banged hard with a bat that rolled along it, then onto the concrete floor where it rattled with a wooden ring. He went back to the rush of darkness he'd just felt, wondering what it would be like to stay blacked out like that for a long time. It was like swimming in the old hot springs with his eyes closed. The boy who had died in the springs when Sea was young had probably felt the same sensation before dying. It was a common but frightening moment after running long distances: the darkness and dulled senses, the effort to come back to normal life, a sensation of bloodless exhaustion and aching, crying muscles. There was not enough oxygen yet pumping into his blood.

What was really happening was homesickness. As he walked back to his dormitory a young woman with black hair passed near him. He thought she looked like Miho, a friend, but she did not seem to see him or hear him when he said hello to her. He realized he was tired and speaking too softly.

As he watched her walk he noticed that her once bright-colored coat had faded with the constant Seattle drizzle. A boy with a dog on a leash passed him, too, and Frank stopped. He watched both figures disappear across campus.

He imagined momentarily that they were war victims. Then he asked himself more soberly, "Why doesn't war touch any of us here at the university?"

He looked eastward. There were several sails on Lake Washington and the Cascade Mountains were white and blue. A gale in the south was razoring its way across the blue sky. The air was fresh and damp. Another drizzle began. Frank kicked a branch off the sidewalk and a dozen grosbeaks flew out of a bush it hit.

*

Dear Brid,

Perhaps this letter will be there for you when you reach Madrid. I miss you and wish spring were already here.

The usual lonely day. Homework. Workouts. Meals in the dining hall. Dorm room bull sessions.

I've held back talking with you about the military because I know it makes you withdraw. I'm not sure why. I'm changing a lot, though, and need to talk with you about it when you can stand it, when you are ready to try to understand what it's like for a guy to face what the war is.

I'm horrified that Don is likely to go to Vietnam. I've learned more about the war than I want to know. I thought about becoming a Conscientious Objector, though don't think I could do it. I've tried that idea out on a few people just to see what the reaction would be. I think most people hate COs more than war protesters. I'm trying to make the best decision based on what I know, but I have no experience to draw upon. I suppose that's why I'm talking with and listening to everybody I can.

I've been reading books by Pascal and Nietzsche. Several nights ago I dreamed a very old man climbed down from the top of the ranchhouse and crawled into my window. He had an odd-looking nose, kind of pointy, but flat underneath like a bloodhound's. He had baggy pants and holey shoes. He introduced himself as "Zarathustra", but frankly he looked a bit like Biscuit Laudon without his hat. He said: "Frank, many go to war, but warriors die. Many go to war, but warriors die happily." Then he climbed out the window and back up onto the roof. Who knows. . . I'm still writing down a lot of dreams. They might mean the opposite of what we think they mean.

If I get a literature or philosophy degree, the military people are not going to be happy about it. They seem to dislike free thinkers of all kinds. They want scientists and engineers, technicians and math wizards.

This summer I want to hike with you. Remember the canyon wall covered with tiny burnt rubies, garnets? Let's go back there. It's amazing that so much beauty can result from fire.

I hope I see Don before he ships out, that is, if he gets drafted as expected. He should know soon. There's another drawing coming up. When I come home next time I'm going to talk with Ron McNiese about the war. I figure a vet like McNiese might have some wisdom I could use, even if he's screwy in other ways. Maybe I'm dead wrong about that. We'll see.

Take care of yourself. Watch out for lecherous Spaniards. Your smile looks at me every day from the picture I have on my desk. I miss you.

Love,
Frank

*

When Frank went to talk with Ron McNiese, he was expecting some neighborly advice, casual advice. He didn't think about or anticipate the rabid side of a war veteran who had been reading about radicals in newspapers and magazines and who had been "born again" as a Christian fundamentalist.

McNiese had been an Air Force pilot during the Korean War. He converted to Christianity when his wife ran off with another man and left him broken-hearted. His nephew had served in Vietnam, had gone into the Army after high school and come back to Idaho a morphine addict. McNiese still thought his nephew had only gone into a detox program for alcohol, and nobody tried to convince him otherwise. He would not have listened.

When Frank drove up to the McNiese residence, Ron saw him coming and stepped outside the house, as if he had been watching from behind the front room curtains and wanted to keep the discussion of Vietnam outside the boundaries of his home. He then jumped eagerly into the car with Frank, ready to talk or preach, whichever might be necessary. Frank hadn't really decided how he was going to approach his conversation with McNiese. It was just going to be a friendly fact-gathering operation, so he thought he might start off talking about some of the CO ideas he was trying to work through.

McNiese's manner was unsettling. He hadn't greeted Frank in the usual way. He seemed distant, a man with a mission. He had the look of a soldier in his eye, a coldness and distance.

"How's school, Frank?" Ron asked, sitting like a mannequin.

"Well, it's going all right."

"What do you want to talk about?"

"Yes. Well. Shall I drive somewhere as we talk? As I said on the phone, I'd appreciate some advice about the military. Percy doesn't know anything about war. He was never in the service, and Emelia doesn't know anything about it either." Snow was collecting on the windshield.

"Sure. Drive somewhere, but not far. I want to spend the evening with my family."

Frank left the car in park. "Basically, I've been doing a lot of thinking about Vietnam. I've been wondering about conscientious objection to the war. I've talked to some people about it and they make some sense."

The remark appeared to upset Ron. He started to breathe heavily, sat up on the edge of the carseat, and looked at Frank with eyes pinched with disgust and nervousness. "I think it's a lie,

Frank. I don't think you're giving *any* thought to being a CO. You aren't sincere. A CO is a COward, nothing else! A yellow coward! Are you telling me you're a coward? You're afraid to fight? We didn't have any room for men like that in the service in my day. We still don't in *my* country. I think you're insincere. I just don't believe you'd choose the way of a coward."

Frank was astonished at the logic: all COs are cowards; you want to be a CO, so you're a coward. He knew being a CO for a particular war had little chance of flying as an argument to get him out of the service. He'd have to be a total CO, like a Mennonite, someone who was against all wars everywhere anytime. While it was true that he didn't think he could be, he still wanted intellectual reassurance somehow that all this 'thinking it through' was worthwhile. He didn't tell Ron that, however. The man was too volatile and hostile.

Ron raised his fist and shook it in Frank's face. "You hear me. You better damned well hear me. If you keep on this path you'll be marching in the streets with niggers soon enough. Bad decisions take us nowhere in life. You'll reneg if you become a CO. I know you will. You will. And I'll make sure a lot of people in this community never have anything to do with you again if you go down that path.

"My nephew was a sergeant over there in Vietnam and I'm proud to death of him. He's a man. He served his country right or wrong. He had guts! Real guts! He took his stand and he'll never be sorry for it. He served when his country called him out. He stayed away from college and all the Communist infiltrators. He considered it philandering with the enemy to go to college."

Frank thought of telling Ron his nephew had been shipped home because he was a drug addict, but thought better of it. Ron's big fist would have put him to sleep for the night.

"We're going to have to start sending troops to campuses in this country pretty soon to keep the Communists out of the classrooms. This country is the best one on earth and it's the best on planet earth because we made it the best in my own day. We've given you young people a great heritage and we're not about to let you send it down the crapper. You sit there at college on your ass eating three squares a day while my nephew is over fighting the enemy: Communist gooks who don't know their ass from a hole in the ground. He cared about his country. It takes a lot of gall for you to come here and tell me you don't believe in the war against Communism! Don't tell me that you think you might be a CO!"

Frank was speechless. He still expected Ron to punch him in the face any moment. The hostility was seething, but all that came out was more invective. He sensed that Ron wanted to hit him, but couldn't quite justify hitting someone who'd asked for his advice. Many people in the community used to make fun of Ron because of his evangelicalism and patriotism. Frank was not laughing at what he was witnessing.

"The Communists have been after this country since the Russian Revolution, Frank. They might get it yet. I hope that through God we're going to keep it from them. They're trying to take us over from within by getting into our schools, into our brains, and don't you doubt that that isn't their objective. People like you have got to get your heads screwed on right! They're after us, Frank. That's a reality you need to know about. They want to destroy our God-fearing nation. They'll be walking up the beaches from landings on the Oregon coast one of these days if people like you can't learn to see the real threat.

"And don't lay any of this 'don't kill innocent mothers and children' crap on me either. When I was in the Korean War I strafed plenty of bivouacs full of women and children. I did what I had to do so that you could be free today, so you could live in a land of liberty, a free nation. I've never had one qualm about having done anything wrong in that war. I'd do it again tomorrow.

"If you quit the service because you say you're a CO over Nam and if that twink of a Catholic preacher in Sandy Crossing writes you a recommendation, I'll see him run out of this state pronto. He tried it once. I'll see that his diocese crucifies him this time. Now. . . I'm going back inside to be with my family because they're what's important to me. Don't contact me again until you get your shit together. I mean it!" Ron jumped out of the car as if it were a boxing ring and he had just won the fight. He slammed the car door.

Frank was stunned. How did McNiese know he might be thinking of getting Tom Petrella's priest to write a letter on his behalf? Maybe the good father had done it for some other man Frank didn't know about yet. Maybe he should find that man and talk to him. And what did black people protesting in the streets have to do with Vietnam? McNiese's racist comment came out of left field entirely and left Frank wondering at the reality the man lived in his head. It was not expected, especially from someone like McNiese who was otherwise disdainful and articulate about the dangers of fascism.

Several days later Frank had a dream that he wrote in his journal:

— Ron McNiese introduced his nephew Chuck to a war veterans' prayer breakfast. Chuck got up in front of everyone and cried with the saddest expression on his face. He seemed broken down and old, and he had an olive complexion, much darker than in real life. His uncle looked at him with these big surprised and disgusted eyes as Chuck concluded his weepy speech with a quote from the warring king at the end of J.R. Tolkien's book The Hobbit. *The king said to Bilbo: "Kindly child of the west, I'm sorry I called you a coward— for you are wiser than I. War is an abomination."*

*

Don threw another log into the stove and shut the iron door. The window was hard to see through because of all the ski equipment cluttering the porch. Nevertheless, Frank could tell it was snowing again. He and Don had another cup of tea.

"I feel like I'm having to defend getting drafted," Don said to Frank.

"Yeah, I'm totally negative about the war now."

"I wish I could be as idealistic as you, but I don't see it the way you do. Peace and war are one. Fighting is a posture you take to keep the two together. If you live during war you fight. If you live during peace you promote harmony. Sure there's evil in war, and wars are different. I don't know how this one started. It doesn't matter, really. We have to trust our leaders to be doing the right thing to a large extent. They must be, right? This is a democracy. There must be a perspective we're not seeing, I figure. I don't agree entirely with Ron McNiese, but he's got some points right. I don't think Communism is good, and I think Communists want to see us ruined.

"If soldiers are good men, they'll be fighting a good cause. I can accept the dangers. Violence is a part of tranquility. It's human nature. It's tied together like male and female."

"That sounds like a mix of all kinds of ideas to justify what you're about to do. You're reading too many different books, and you've been reading too much of the *I Ching*.

"I am starting to think that the colonialism that lingered in Southeast Asia has a lot to do with the current situation. Those people were trying to shake the colonial bit and, lo and behold, the Americans show up to thank the Marquis de Lafayette by taking over their military operations. History is bizarre. Instead of helping the Vietnamese realize that they could establish a real democracy, America goes in and props up an old neo-colonial state. They drive the Vietnamese into the silly communist matrix and Shazamm! All of a sudden we've got a dumb war and American political bigots running it."

"Well, The *I Ching* sure is a different book; it just makes sense to me."

"I think you're joining up for a change, Don. I don't think you believe in the war. You're really unhappy and you want to forget that unhappiness."

"The foreign legion motive?"

"Yeah, I guess so. You've been so unhappy this past year, especially since your father died."

Don was surprised by Frank's comment, but not offended. "You mean you think I have a death wish, or something like that?"

"Don, nothing is that subtle. Of course not. Here I am talking to you about your depression. What a switch, huh?"

"Well, Frank, I won't hide it. You know me well enough. I can't say there isn't something that makes me want to get the hell out of Crawford's Nook. It's hard being an only child, especially when you lose a parent. Mom wants to die now. She actually says so. She misses my father so much. It doesn't say a lot about my source of inspiration, that she'd want to stay around because her son needs her. Any loneliness I already felt has been pretty well compounded. I hardly have a single relative. And the last steady girlfriend I had was in tenth grade. I get angry. I get cruel, to myself, for sure."

Don rocked in the chair in front of the fire, boots propped on a log drying. Frank thought he'd said too much. Even Don, it seemed, liked being a victim sometimes.

"Frank, I know what I'm doing. By the way, do you still think about God much?"

Frank seemed surprised by the question. He hadn't talked about religion, God, or faith with Don for years. "I think it's background, Don. It's always there like the mountains at the end of the valley, but I don't try to sort it out much anymore. I had too many arguments with my mother, and Percy and Madge never discussed such things. I think mostly of good and right direction, and I hope I have the courage to do what's right before I die so I don't have to end up with a lot of regrets before they push me into the channel in a canoe. Who's the big guy and what's my relationship there? No, I avoid thinking about that kind of thing. The religious people who have a grid they run everything through are wrong. I think there's something else when we die, and somehow we continue on. In the end, it doesn't really matter what I think because my brain's going to turn to dust. I suppose there's an essence to me, the good energy of a guy named Frank, a faint flash or twinkle that can be seen in the dark, that will go on in a nice incandescent way, and not just in somebody else's memory. If I live a good life I'll pulse a lot stronger than if I live a bad one."

"Frank, that's good to know about you. There are some good thoughts there."

Frank was at a barrier. No remorse accompanied his having questioned Don. The fire crackled. Don took out his harmonica and played a variation on a **Country Joe and the Fish** song. Frank lifted the stove door handle and tossed a split chunk of tamarack into the firebox.

When Don put down the harmonica Frank asked, "Do you have any yellow ski wax on you?"

"Oh, yeah. I brought you a bar." Don got up and handed the bar to Frank, then Frank put on his coat.

"I've got to get going. I'll see you tomorrow before I do the disappearing thing again."

"Let me know if that color works. It should be right for this texture of snow and the snow's not going to change much by tomorrow. You'll sail along that track."

*

The Journal Frank kept was undated. It contained fragments of dreams, observations, quotes, messages to himself, snippets of philosophy and metaphysics, ideas. It was ungainly because it was composed of paper fragments dropped into manila folders, lined and unlined paper, yellow legal pad paper, napkins, index cards, writing squeezed into margins of torn pages, programs, receipts, or matchbooks. He leafed through it under the category of "religion and values" and read the following entries and scraps:

— Some preachers take characters from the Christian Bible and turn them into metaphors. Several weeks ago Rev. Richards at the Unitarian Church said that Zaccheus, a rich tax collector, represented the American economy. The message, he said, is social justice.

— Rev. Walmsby of the Presbyterian Church is a Wycliffe Bible Translator who believes that he must put the Christian gospel into every imaginable tongue so that the 'marriage of the lamb' might take place. This strange consummation, which is to take place between Jesus and the Church, will not occur until 'every tongue confesses the gospel.' His view is that he, personally, is 'holding up' the marriage by not working faster, harder.

— Who was Jesus anyway? The orthodox Christians say: both God and human, a blend of transcendent and immanent. The Docetists say: only transcendent God. Kazantzakis saw Jesus as the man, the immanent but chosen one. Schweitzer considered Jesus a psychotic but great moral teacher. The popular view: Jesus was one of many messengers, the best of those sent, the greatest prophet. Bonhoeffer viewed him as the image for regenerative character development, the one who cared only for others. Tillich saw a historic symbol by which one could find meaning. Chardin

had a unique postulation: Jesus is the great cosmic and universal reference point for all evolution.

— Christians talk of calling. Is there really anything to this? Should calling not just be seen as a gift of one's life, a given life? Isn't 'being' calling?

— Faith is always just one fin ahead of the shark of despair. Sometimes it is in the shark's jaws, pinned by arrowheads of teeth.

— Good King Wenceslaus wore a hair shirt.

— I saw a plaster of Paris St. Francis of Assisi in one of my professors' homes. It was holding paper clips.

— The morality of right-wing Christians seems greatly akin to fascism. Wait till the anti-war radicals take over; we'll see the antithetical side of fascism and it won't be that different.

— The power of otherness/godness/noumena comes like a nature force. It cannot be prevented. It carries one away.

— Concepts seem to force themselves upon us. Concepts are as close as one can get to godness. Is this Platonism?

— Faith is an attitude, an atmosphere, a way of behavior.

— My two monk friends at the monastery near the university: Father Basil is thin and has creases around his eyes like cartwheels of sunshine. Father Demetri is built like a bull. His cheeks are lined with boulders. They're both cobblers who fix shoes for free.

— All this trying to "be one with God" seems to lead to being totally alone.

— I think one quality is required to be a Christian evangelist: blindness.

— In love: persevere, be yourself, don't compare yourself with others.

— Tolerance, courage, humor, trust, sincerity, and honesty must displace moroseness, smugness, vanity, blindness, infidelity, and petty dishonesty.

— Nathaniel West introduced into a secular setting the 'idea' of embracing the unlovely.

— Introspection is a difficult, precarious art.

— *Love is not something humans do. It's something divine that courses through us sometimes during our lives. We do not do it. It finds us, possesses us.*

— *Pascal didn't think much of death: "The last act is tragic, however happy all the rest of the play is; at the last a little earth is thrown upon our head, and that is the end forever."*

St. Christopher

"Well, it wouldn't hurt to go see him, Frank. Your mother is so set on helping you. This is one way she can feel she's done her duty. Father Haswell is decent. I met him one day in the shop. Since you won't see a Protestant minister, he's the only Catholic for nearly a hundred miles. A couple of the boys in his parish went to Vietnam. I'm sure he's thought and prayed a lot about the war.

If you decide to be one of those conscience objectors, you'll need the signature of a clergyman anyway."

"It's *conscientious objector*, Beullah, and I'm not sure I'm going to do that."

"Well, talking to the man will do you good. The more perspective you have, the better, right?"

"I don't want this to rile up people around here. I know Dick Petrella is a member of that parish. He's a gung-ho war vet like Ron McNiese. If any of the vets at that church are close to McNiese, he could make it difficult on Fr. Haswell if he signs a CO form for me."

"You should go talk to Ron. He might just understand your viewpoint."

"Beullah, I already did. I talked to him. If I had looked at him cross-eyed he would have beat the living daylights out of me."

"No, not Ron McNiese. He's not a violent person, not since he stopped drinking."

"Yes, McNiese. Everyone in this community thinks of him and his religion as a kind of clown show. Well, he's a vet, a nasty one. He doesn't believe anything half-heartedly. He's a true believer, a fanatic. War's no different. He actually told me that communists, propaganda, and *niggers* were behind why I question the war."

162

"Did he really say nigger?"

"You bet he did."

Beullah was silent for a few moments. Then she said, "Frank, lots of good people are beginning to doubt the validity of the war. A war isn't supposed to drag on the way it is over there. There's something wrong. Every evening before supper we have to listen to the death toll on television. You follow your instincts, Frank. Don't let McNiese frighten you. He's a little off in the head, but I didn't know he was prejudiced against black folk."

Just then Emelia came in the back door to the shop. "Whoooh! That snow is getting deep. We'll all be buried by the end of the month. The Chamber of Commerce will have to call in the National Guard to dig us out."

Beullah said to Frank, "You can find Haswell at his office in Sandy Crossing in the afternoons. It won't hurt you to go talk with him. He's a very smart man, I hear."

"My minister will talk with you, Frank," said Emelia.

"I know, Mother. I don't want to talk with him. You know that. I already spoke with Ron McNiese and your minister and McNiese are tight friends. They see things exactly alike."

"Well, they're brothers in Christ."

"Yes, Mother, *bros.* in Christ. I'll see you ladies later."

"There's no reason to be smart, Frank."

*

When Frank drove up, Fr. Haswell was shoveling snow in front of the two-room Catholic Church. He was in Levis, Roman collar, a green stocking cap, and snowmobiler boots. Frank introduced himself and Haswell acknowledged that someone in his parish had told him "the Ravan boy" might come down to have a guidance chat. Haswell had a southwestern drawl, probably Texan or Oklahoman, Frank conjectured.

"Come on inside, Frank, would you like a cup of tea or coffee?"

"Oh, no thanks."

"The Petrellas talk about you sometimes."

"Well, I grew up with Tom."

"They said you are in college. Are you studying anything in particular?"

"Not yet. I'm just trying to get through the Vietnam phase, I guess. I like reading."

"Have you read *The Divine Comedy*?"

"*The Inferno* is part of that, right?"

"Yes. So you have read some of Dante?"

"Love that moves the worlds and starry powers. . . or something like that, right?"

"Yes, that's it. Poetry's a comfort to me, as is the Bible. So what can I help you with?"

Frank looked around the small side office that doubled as a sacristy. "I guess I'm looking for help in making a decision about Vietnam. My grandfather is not a war veteran and doesn't really have an opinion on the matter. My father passed away when I was young and he wasn't a vet either. I've met some ex-GIs at college and they talk like the war is worse than *The Inferno*. I'm in Navy ROTC and am supposed to fly jets in a few years, and I'm getting concerned that I won't be able to bring myself to go to war when the time comes."

"So you haven't been drafted?"

"Oh, no."

"You joined ROTC out of your own free will?"

"Yes."

"Do you feel this is an obligation?"

"Yes, I do. I also feel I may have made a bad decision and a commitment I can't keep."

"So you don't think you can keep your commitment?"

"Not 'can keep'. It's more like: I now don't want to keep the commitment."

"That is, indeed, a problem. When we make commitments, we must endeavor to keep them. If we cannot keep them we must seek God's forgiveness for violating a trust. Have you endeavored to keep this commitment? When you enrolled in the scholarship program was there anything you didn't know that justifies you quitting now?"

"I think I have tried to keep my commitment, but I've learned so much. I feel like I made a decision before I had enough information."

"Were you forced? By whom, Frank?"

"Well, okay. I probably made a mistake by making the commitment. No one forced me."

"It doesn't matter what your motives were. I assume you wanted financial aid for school?"

"Yes, mostly. Plus I wanted to fly. Don't we all want to fly? Isn't it human nature somehow to want to just go up on the roof or the window ledge and jump into the wind like a bird and soar away?"

"I suppose it is, Frank. You seem to understand yourself. This is not an issue of self-knowledge, is it? How can I help you?"

"I suppose I want assurance, and if I decide I'm a conscientious objector I will need the signature of a clergyman."

"I see. Are you a Christian?"

"I was raised that way and baptized."

"You're not a Catholic?"

"No."

"Well, for me to sign a paper when you're not in my care would be going out on a limb. The Church doesn't encourage it."

Frank had a memory of O'Seetley's hot springs where he had been dipped under the water as a boy, then blessed with some sacred platitudes by a Protestant minister. The hot springs pond near the Notch was used for many purposes including parties, picnics, and baptisms.

Frank visualized the springs for a moment, when no one was around except Sea and himself. Its warm pond was crowded with cattle that favored eating a particular kind of grass that grew in the shallows. Children typically avoided going into the shallows because they were mined with cow pies, covered with rushes and cattails, and also were home to gigantic bullfrogs, toads, and water snakes. Sea liked to catch toads and carry them around with him while he and Frank swam. Frank remembered a huge toad that Sea slipped into the water next to the minister when Frank was about to be baptized. The minister gave it a judo chop and ran out of the water momentarily. Sea's father, Russell, ran down to the water and pulled Sea out of the pool by the ear. He slapped him on the rump, but neither Sea nor Frankie could stop laughing for several minutes.

On Frankie's baptismal day all the children to be baptized stepped around the cow mature and salt blocks that were irregularly eroded by cattle saliva into dirty white jadeite forms. After the toad ruckus the children waded out to meet the minister who was wearing a white cotton gown.

Percy often told people later that on the day his grandson Frankie had been 'symbolically buried with Christ' he had seen an unusual number of water snakes slithering over the surface of the hot springs pond along with the giant toad Sea had carried to the minister. Emelia and Madge always got upset with Percy when he told this story and glowered at him until he desisted. Percy would then wink at Sea.

Fr. Haswell continued, "At the time of your baptism were you sure of your salvation?"

"I prayed to Jesus before I went under the water. I did everything right, I think, everything I was told, that is. I think I would just like the comfort of knowing I have done things as right as possible. We never know where our decisions will take us, but knowing we make the best judgment possible with the information at hand, that is important to me. The Petrellas all have great confidence in you, Father, and I have always wanted to be comfortable with a minister of the Christian faith. My family's background in Protestantism is only possible because of Catholicism, and I know there should just be one faith. I don't understand why Protestants persist in peeling away from one another. Once they all started 'dissenting', it had no end to it. My mother's friends are all members of Protestant groups that think they are each right, and they really dislike each other. Worse, they malign each other. *Anyhoo*, I guess I have looked forward to talking with you because deep inside I find a desire to speak honestly, openly, and be brave enough to hear the voice of someone 'of the cloth' who might tell me something that rings true but is hard to accept. "

"Frank, your soul's jeopardy is more important than the decisions made during ten Vietnams."

"I'm just thinking that my soul will be in jeopardy if I don't get out of the Navy, or at least try to. I'll be forced to drop bombs on people I have no knowledge of. That can't be right, can it?"

"Frank, God can be with you wherever you are, whatever you're doing. Men in the military can know God. There's never enough information for military men to always avoid inflicting havoc on the unfortunate. They must do their best, of course, but it is not always easy and they sometimes have to depend on their faith. They pray that they will not be part of an operation that is ill-designed or wrongheaded. I know this may sound like casuistry, but I know it to be the case. I have stories from faithful, praying soldiers and sailors who have discovered after they have done their duty that they had somehow avoided being parties to appalling deeds."

Frank was growing uneasy. He was afraid of just having another highbrow conversation about military ethics. He had had too many of these discussions, and usually his conclusions at the end were tormenting. He didn't really know this man. His gentleness seemed uncertain. The priest also seemed preoccupied with something Frank knew nothing about: a meeting or obligation, etc. Frank disliked the fact that he was beginning to feel judgmental toward this man of God. It also made him feel uncomfortable.

"Father Haswell, despite my mistakes, I feel it might be the right thing for me to exit the Navy program. To do so though, I have to have a reason. The Government requires me to provide them with a good reason, and there's a formula behind what they think is a good reason."

"Is that because of your commitment?"

"Yes."

"Something else is important here, Frank. Is your conviction about needing to get out of the Navy based on what you think, or on what God says to you through prayer?"

"Well, Vietnam is not mentioned in the Bible, but many other questionable wars are. Some of them seem to have been supported by the Hebrew God."

"The Hebrew God? Are you suggesting that you really believe in polytheism.

"Well, that wasn't my point. I meant that maybe we're not getting all the facts about some of those wars if we're just reading what's in the Bible."

"So you think the Bible has some obvious biases?"

"I didn't say biases. I might say incompletions."

"You think the Bible is incomplete?"

"Yes."

"Based on my studies and vocational training it is complete enough for spiritual guidance, Frank. It only has in it what we *need* to know."

"Well, if that's the case, can you show me something that's relevant to what I'm going through, and what a lot of others like me are going through? I haven't seen anything in there that reminds me of Vietnam."

"Frank, to put the matter quite straight, the only thing that would justify your objection to the Vietnam War would be for you to prove that for you to obey your government, for you to serve your country, would be equivalent to disobeying God. All that I read in Scripture about war and government expresses uncompromisingly that the best way for all of us to obey God is usually through obeying the civil authorities that we— through our contracts with them— put over us. It pleases God when He sees us obeying these authorities He's established over us for our own good. Do you sincerely disagree with me about this?"

Frank felt he'd reached a dead-end, the one he didn't want to reach. It wasn't being forced on him but he felt he might be there. He had genuinely hoped Fr. Haswell would help him in some unexpected way. Now he was thinking he might have just approached the situation in the wrong way.

"Thank you for your time, Father," he said. "I appreciate your spending some time with me. I'll tell the Petrellas I was able to speak with you. I did hear through the grapevine that you might have helped someone else get out of the service with a letter supporting CO status."

"I'm not, unfortunately, at liberty to discuss that with you, Frank. My bishop has asked me not to. The circumstances were particular. I wish I could be more helpful, Frank."

"I know."

Frank had a dream the next night and wrote in his journal:

— Father Haswell and I are speaking. I say to him, "The problem with the Church is that I'm off schedule. On Good Friday I'm having a blast, and on Easter morning I'm ready to blow my brains out."

*

Upset over the conversation he'd had with Ron McNiese, Frank told Percy about it. His grandfather was sitting in his usual armchair, just awakened from a nap. Percy could sometimes still focus fairly clearly. He didn't like McNiese intimidating his grandson.

"You're smart, Frank. Take what McNiese had to say with a grain of salt. Remember, there's a good reason why his wife ran off some years back. He can be a real jerk; but like all of us, his butt points at the ground. Too much religion, babble about the importance of family values, and patriotism can lead one to idiocy. Remember that old hunting buddy of McNiese's who talked to you years ago at the Crawford's Nook picnic? He told you what McNiese was really like: having to haul him out of the flee-bitten, dingy whorehouses of Manila or Okinawa after the war. Remember that? That made a whole lot of sense to me when I found out.

"Also, McNiese was in one of those night bomber groups. His squadron didn't have any direct contact with the enemy. They just flew over their targets in total darkness and released their payloads when a gauge needle flickered correctly in the darkness. He never saw any suffering. He never faced any accidents or firestorms that he caused. He could never have been sure he always dropped bombs on the right targets. How could he have been? All McNiese ever did in that Korean War was steer a plane in the right direction and pull levers about twice a week."

*

Coming through town Frank ran into Ron McNiese's nephew. He asked Chuck how he was doing and he replied that he'd been home for several months. Frank asked, "Did you see any action?"

"Not really," Chuck admitted, "none at all, in fact. I know my uncle likes to brag about me, but I worked in a warehouse near Saigon. It never came close to getting anything incoming."

Frank wanted to ask the big question and finally did, "Say, I hear you were using smack for a while."

Chuck answered the question politely and plainly, without hesitating. He was not embarrassed. He was aware there had already been a lot of gossip in the county about him and he was a truthful person with nothing to hide at this point in his life. He said, "Look, Frank, doing that kind of thing is really the only way to get through your tour. Everyone over there is on dope and as crazy as a shithouse rat."

*

Frank sat in the office lobby and waited for the commander to call him in. The secretary sat behind her desk, typing a letter. She wore a string of white pearls that disappeared into a ravine between abundant breasts. In her mid-thirties, a few wrinkles were beginning to appear beneath her eyes. A heavy smoker, her lips were starting to cone and yellow. You could tell she carried most of the burdens of the commander's administration, but her office was barely big enough for filing cabinets and a desk, let alone a set of chairs for a waiting area.

Several times she got up and walked to the filing cabinets to file forms, a mere step and half. As she did this she twisted herself past the electric typewriter that stuck out the side of the desk on a small diving board. Each time that she leaned forward over the typewriter with correction tape, blond bangs like little wings hovered over the sides of large white glass frames. As she sat back again, they pivoted clear of the frames.

A picture of the Da Nang Air Force Base in Vietnam hung on the wall above her desk and on an adjacent wall next to the commander's office door was a poster of Navy jets being refueled above a snowy Japanese volcano. "Join the U.S. Navy and see the World" the poster said in red, white and blue. Frank remembered a radical poster someone had pasted on a wall in his dormitory. It said, "Join the U.S. Navy, See People from all over the World and Kill Them."

Frank sat next to the commander's door in his best pair of cotton slacks, an open-collared black knit shirt, and well-worn hiking boots and wool socks. Over his knee he held a blue denim jacket with a frayed waistband and a yellow notepad. After about fifteen minutes the intercom buzzed, "Send him in, Debbie."

"He'll see you now," she said to Frank, who had already stood to go in.

Frank turned and opened a tall, thick white door that swung into one corner of the room. In contrast to the secretary's area, the room seemed as large as a ballroom. At the far end there was a wide bay window over twelve feet tall and under it a large desk. Frank had seen the room once before, when he had been sworn in with seven other pilot candidates. The commander's wooden desk reminded him of a judge's bench. To the left was an eight-foot tall American flag and pole. The commander sat behind the desk, a man in blue who reminded Frank of a retired Chicago Bears lineman. He had a crewcut and golden brown eyes that focused perfectly. Frank felt like saying to the commander, "Hello *there!*" or "Hello *over there!*" Instead, he marched toward the commander's desk, came to attention, saluted and reported-in a few paces in front of the desk. "Cadet Frank Ravan requesting permission to speak with you, Sir!"

The commander routinely rose to salute saying, "Permission granted, Ravan. Take that chair." The officer returned to his seat, folded his large red hands on the desktop, placed elbows on the desk, then rested his chin on his hands. "So what's on your mind, Ravan?"

Frank sat down next to the desk, perspiring heavily out of nervousness. "Sir, I've wanted to talk with you for some time, but only now have I decided I must." He looked at the floor in front of the chair. He knew his words must sound awkward.

"Sounds important. Get it out, Midshipman!" said the commander, his eyes blazing at Frank. "Say what you have on your mind. You don't have to be formal."

"Well, it's about my contract with the Navy, Sir. I've been bothered with Vietnam for a long time now. I'm not coming to tell you that I'm a conscientious objector or anything exactly like that, but I am coming to say that I believe the war in Vietnam is not on the right track and that I'm no longer willing to serve in the Navy just because I signed a contract. I don't think it's in the Navy's best interest to keep me on as a pilot candidate."

The commander's brows dipped in attitude and it seemed to Frank that there was a spark in the pupils. He didn't say a word, but just looked at Frank, who finally looked away and out the window for a few moments. As Frank turned, however, he still felt the heat of the commander's gaze. He was sweating in silence as the commander maintained the stare. About five minutes passed. Frank focused his eyes on an elm tree out the office window. It was beginning to rain. Frank wished he were standing under the cool rain outside instead of sitting in the hot seat near the commander awaiting his response.

The commander, of course, had a purpose in not speaking, but Frank did not know it. Frank waited as patiently as he could for the commander to say something, but still he did not.

Finally, out of the silence, as if a machine gun were being fired, the commander began to shout. "Is that all you wanted to say, Frank Ravan? Is that all you wanted to say to me and to the Navy of the United States of America, Cadet Ravan?"

Frank nearly fell off his chair, wincing. His face and shoulder muscles twitched. "Sir!" he stammered, "I am not declaring myself a CO. I am just saying that I don't think the Navy is going to benefit from my service. My heart is not in this. Engineers don't direct bands, cowboys don't ride pigs, and insurance salesmen don't do dental work. To force me to go through with this program in the Navy will be forcing a square block into a round hole. I can't believe I didn't understand myself well enough before starting college to recognize this is not going to work. I wasn't made for it, to fit in, that is; that's all I'm saying. I've thought a lot about this. I want to be honest about it. I have serious moral issues with this war. I can't solve the problem of the war, but I can stop participating in something I don't believe in. The war has no direction. It's not being won. It's not being lost. It's like a sailing ship drifting in the horse latitudes."

"Cadet, we are not made to fit in. None of us are made to *fit*. We fit ourselves into doing what's necessary." The commander rose from his chair and leaned over his desk, almost poking his nose into Frank's face. "You say you want to be honest, Cadet? You haven't said anything honest yet. Self-centered people can't be honest. You think you're honest. Ha!" The commander turned and walked to the window, laughing further at Frank; then he walked back and let his words roll out.

"All you care about is yourself, Frank Ravan. Everything you've said to me has only you in mind. Your only concern is for your own skin, your own hopes and dreams. The men who go to war only have others in mind. They sacrifice themselves for others, give themselves to others, sometimes even die for others.

"I flew over sixty missions in Vietnam, was shot down and rescued twice; I spent two years away from my wife and children. But I did it so fellows like you might be able to study and work and enjoy freedom. I gave myself for others, sacrificed myself, prayed on lonely nights before missions. I did it just for you, for you and all the joy you hope to have one day in this life in this country.

"I can see, Cadet, that you have let your pride get in the way of your duty. And that's a disgraceful thing to let happen.

"I'll tell you what. We're all allowed to have one big gaffe apiece in our military careers. If you like, I'll let you walk right out of here now and will forget this episode forever— write it off, erase it— I'll forget you ever came in here today, if you'll forget it, too. But if you insist on letting pride overpower you, then I'll have to force you to accept the consequences of your actions. And they are severe, very severe, Cadet! Do you understand me? You could be on a plane to Vietnam in weeks, or court-martialed and sent to the brig."

"Yes, Sir!"

Another silence settled in and lasted several minutes. Finally Frank broke it, saying, "Sir, I thought seriously about this for a long time before coming in here. This wasn't flip." As he said this he looked down at the parquet floor. He felt very small and wondered that his legs could touch the floor. He wanted to swing them under him like a child and have the commander come scrub his head with the palm of his hand. He wanted to shrink even smaller until he was no longer there, until he became a spot on the chair. He wanted to run away, to get away from this situation, to forget forever the commander, B-52's, Phantoms, SAMs, Hound-dog Missiles, and Vietnam Air Bases. This, he realized, was the worst moment he had ever experienced. He thought he was trying to do the right thing, yet here he was offending one of his country's leading patriots.

Momentarily, Frank recalled his philosophy readings for the week. Pascal's father had warned him against his growing pride. In Plato's dialogues Socrates' enemies said he had become a "monster of pride." Frank tried to leverage his way in there between Pascal and Socrates, but knew he didn't fit. It was a pathetic exercise in trying to hold onto ideals that were bigger than he was. It just made him feel worse.

"So you thought seriously about this for a long time, did you? You're just like other misguided students these days, students who believe what they want to believe, who do what they want to do, who throw off all their obligations and responsibilities like so much rubbish. I don't believe you're any different than the rest of the ilk going through our educational institutions these days. Only you have the audacity to throw it up in my face after you've signed a military contract!"

Frank's heart was beating right out of his chest. He felt as though someone were hitting him rhythmically in the head with fists. He wanted to cry out, to disappear, to fight back, but instead he sat there doing nothing. His face was expressionless. He went inward, toppling back into himself, down into his soul, further and further, head over heels.

He hoped to hit the bottom when all of a sudden he experienced a floating sensation like floating on a summer lake in an inner tube. Around and around he went in the tube, dizzyingly plunging over waterfalls into blackness after blackness. After floating downward for several minutes he hit a stone bottom that took his breath away. It was cold. He felt the surface with his hands, but there was still blackness all around him. Dust began to blow into his face and nostrils. He tried to breath. He tried to lie still and press his body firmly against the stone.

Then, as though awaking from a dream, he spoke to the commander. It was not an oracle, but the best he could do. The words came easily because there was nothing else Frank thought he could do except open his mouth and let out whatever words came naturally. "Sir, how can you say those things to me when you don't really know me? I am the only one who knows whether what I say reflects truth or not. You have no right to say what you said about pride or cowardice. I am the only one who knows what I am. And maybe I am wrong. Maybe I am a coward, but I do not see it that way at this time, during this instance. Maybe I am proud; in fact, you are probably right. I think I am trying, however, to see how I might be hurting other people. I've thought so long and hard about this that I'm just tired of it all. I'm exhausted with worrying over it. I might be wrong, but this war is crazy. Even you have got to admit that."

The commander was silent.

"Everything I've learned from men coming back from the war— the ones who are willing to talk about it— tells me that something is wrong over there. In fact, something is wrong over here. We're living out a disaster. I don't think all the students demonstrating are right. They may be very wrong in many ways. I'm just trying to visualize where I fit in. This can't be what enlisting in WW II was like for the men who wanted to protect their country. It just can't be! Did you enlist in WW II? Was it like this?"

The commander's lips parted about half an inch as he tilted backwards in his rocking desk chair. Frank watched him push back as he spoke, as if he held an oar in his hands and was pushing away from a dock. The commander stared.

Frank turned his eyes back toward the rain on the elm tree's thick gray trunk. Light green leaves dripped rainwater onto the windowsill and rain spattered loudly against a windowpane. A car splashed through water in the street outside and below the office.

"So you're dead set against the Navy, are you?" asked the commander, finally with a hint of resignation, leaning back into his desk again. Some of the fire seemed gone from his eyes now. "You just don't want to go to war? You've got two weeks to think about it. Then come back and we'll talk again if you like."

Frank could hardly believe the change in the commander's tone of voice. 'He is giving me a little space to breathe then?' he asked himself. 'I'm saved for the moment? I'm not being shipped out to Vietnam as a Midshipman next week?'

"I've spent more time with you than I can afford," the commander continued. "I've got important work to do. Come back in two weeks if you'd like."

Frank stood up, unsure if his legs would hold him. He came to attention a few feet away from his chair. "Cadet Frank Ravan requesting permission to leave, Sir."

"Dismissed!" said the commander loudly as he saluted.

Frank walked briskly toward the door, but after turning the crystal doorknob and pulling it open several inches the commander's voice caught up with him again. "By the way, Ravan, forget about what I said to you about pride in shirking your duty. You've done well as a cadet around here up till now. I say that thing about pride to all my men when I think they're out of line."

Frank was surprised as he looked back toward the commander, then slightly relieved. He looked out the window, then alternately at the commander. After another silent moment, the commander, realizing Frank was staring at him, shouted again, "Dismissed, Cadet!"

Frank left the room and passed the picture of Da Nang Air Force Base on his left. He said nothing to the secretary whose face indicated that she was not used to hearing the commander shout from inside his office. She looked at Frank as if to ask, "What in God's name did you say to him anyway?"

*

The room thumped like a huge heart. He remembered the woman who seemed intent on seducing him. She wore a tight red dress hiked up high on her thighs until he could see the most mesmerizing chevron of lacy black panties.

"Get up, get up!" someone kept saying. He tried to stand up but something bumped his head. He was under a table. He finally made it to his feet and a rush of black filled his brain, then a chunk of yellow light came toward him and he found himself accelerating, then tumbling across grass.

Someone touched his shoulder. He opened his eyes. It was her: the *Zucker-zange* with the black lingerie. "Are you used to drinking? You're in fine shape, my friend," she said.

"My rudder's broken."

"Ah, you're a sailor?"

"I've sailed some, yes."

"Listen, let me help you. We can walk to my place. It's two blocks."

As Frank looked at the young woman, darkness seeped back into his brain. Soon he was watching a white boat's prow burst through a blue-gray lake swell. The glare of sun was strong. The sky was deep blue.

He woke up looking into a hedge. Dew had soaked his clothes. He looked at his watch and it was four a.m. He walked back to his dorm room and took a shower.

Coming back from the shower to his room he took several aspirin, drank a quart of water, then leafed through his journal under the category 'social stresses'. He added the following

entries:

— *The American economy is a war economy.*

— *For every one who learns to rise from poverty, another is born into the mess.*

— *Last summer I took my Indian crew on a forest fire fighting trip to Ely, Nevada. Flew to Elko, slept at the Forest Service dispatch office, had breakfast at the Commercial Hotel, met a bunch of Sioux Indians, Pete chopped up a rattlesnake while beating out the flames of a little flare-up, had another meal at the Commercial Hotel, then waited for some of the crew before flying back after the fire. They were visiting one of Nevada's finest whorehouses. I wouldn't let my Indian crew go there.*

— *Talked with Daniel Ellsberg, who is writing a book about the Pentagon, and Lowell Weicker, a traveling politician, who visited campus. Ellsberg said nuclear weapons are unsafe to handle, that Gen. Westmoreland has considered using a nuclear charge in Vietnam, and that the Cuban Missile Crisis was a sham to whip up support for more nuclear weapons. Weicker said America has to have a complete nuclear arsenal or else be destroyed by the Soviet Union.*

— *My friend from the fraternity showed me pictures of Peru where he went to help people who had been in a terrible earthquake. A valley was full of bright brown alluvium and thousands of people were buried beneath it.*

— *From the Christian Bible, Revelations 9:2: "When he unlocked the shaft of the abyss, smoke poured up out of the abyss like the smoke from a huge furnace so that the sun and sky were darkened by it." 6:14: "The sky disappeared like a scroll rolling up and all the mountains and islands were shaken from their places."*

The world's end by fire? The Japanese of Hiroshima, indeed, endured hell on earth. They must have thought, 'if there is hell, we're in it: people walking nowhere, imprints of vaporized bodies on objects, death sickness ahead.'

We live in an age of fear. There is not really peace, for there is no place to escape the threat of nuclear war. Nuclear plant workers insist they must feed their families. On Hiroshima Day in Seattle Japanese school children make thousands of paper cranes, small hands offering an alternative to nuclear industry employment.

— Another university football game and the sexually liberated culture of the 60s and 70s offered fans yet another halftime display about the relationship between sex and war. Today the stadium is overflowing. A "Thanks Sports Lovers!" balloon heads into the sky, cheered by thousands of fans in parkas and tweed coats. The band gives a marching sexual interpretation of history: A pyramid has a "hardened" center, a medieval maiden is unchaste, a stiff kick is delivered to workers to get their "masses" in gear. Then the finale: a stubby pillar explodes at the top into a mushroom cloud: the bomb. Drunken laughter and cheering. Cheerleaders are groped and passed up the stands above the heads and arms of cheering fans.

— A militant publication my roommate lent me says that America has spent $144,000 per enemy dead in Vietnam. The $5,000 of an NROTC scholarship goes to a better purpose when compared with that.

— A 1,400 mph Phantom jet comes sweeping in at low altitude through a tight canyon— trees shaking, dishes and windows rattling— and drops two canisters of napalm that flare the jungle into white and yellow flame and billowing dark smoke. The jet rolls and disappears straight into the sun. What is it about this scene that makes a young man want to do it? The noise? The destruction? The assumed courage? The technical skill of flying? The insignia on the jet? The fact that it's flying at supersonic speed? Grasping that life under Communistic rule would be worse?

SPRING FEVER

Pleased with his effort on the pre-calculus midterm, all Frank could think about for hours afterwards was the mystery of the indivisibility of zero. The grass on the lawn by the observatory was still white with snow, but he wanted spring so badly that he imagined what it had been like a year earlier. The lawn was green, the wisteria dark lavender, and the tulips yellow and black.

On the walkway he met Miho, who had been in his art class. A native Filipino with some Japanese family background, she had black hair that covered her back like a wet, sunlit sea otter hide.

"Miho?" he said, coming up behind her.

She spun a hundred and eighty degrees and stopped. Her hair kept going. "Oh, Hi Frank. I haven't seen you on campus for a few moons."

"I know. I'm staying out of traffic, trying to keep everything in perspective. You still in the sorority and taking those drawing classes?"

"Yes, I'm still working on lines, but I'm moving off campus soon. You're a runner, aren't you?"

"I compete in cross country."

"I've been jogging regularly with my roommate. My grandfather says it's good for my young heart."

"Would you like to run sometime? There are several terrific loops I could show you: sound-to-mountain-and-lake-and-back kinds of things."

"Yes, I'd like to do that, Frank."

"So is your grandfather a runner?"

"A swimmer. Still swims every day or two. He's eighty-eight. Lives in Hilo, Hawaii now. He says I should run barefoot to stay connected to the earth. He used to do it as a boy in the trails around our home in the Philippines."

"That would be tough around here. Has he ever lived in a city?"

"Well, no. I suppose not, probably not even Manila. The closest he ever got was to Honolulu harbor where, for a while, he was a crewman on a barge that unloaded palm trees."

"What were they doing with palm trees."

"They take them from the Big Island and Maui to other islands for the resorts."

"You mean they cut them down like fir trees?"

"Well, not exactly."

"But it's a commodity like logs for lumber? I never heard of using palm lumber."

"Well, it's not the same. The trees are living. They're living logs. They plant them."

"I see. So the trees get planted, like nursery trees with roots wrapped in burlap and vermiculite?"

"Yes, that's the idea."

"Miho, I have to be at the fieldhouse in a few minutes. May I call you sometime?"

"Sure, anytime; here's my number. I'll write it on your notebook. I'd love to go jogging. By the way, would you model for me sometime?"

"Model?"

"Yes, I'd like to draw your portrait."

"No one's ever asked me to do that before."

"Oh well, enjoy the notoriety. Charcoal is what I'd like to use."

"Yes, sure. Why not? I'll be your poster boy."

Several days later Frank got up the courage to call Miho and arranged to meet her at a studio in the art school so that she could do his sketch. After finishing her first outline they went running. Four weeks later Frank shared a poem with her. He read it to her one afternoon while she was struggling with the light in the portrait. Frustrated and massaging the portrait with a giant eraser, she had stopped work momentarily and asked him to read her the poem.

He declined and suggested she read it by herself. He said, "I don't want that kind of an introduction for my writing. I'm not good at reading, that is, reading to someone who's never read anything of mine before. It may not ring true for you, or you might not understand it exactly the way I intended. That always makes me nervous when I share my writing."

She picked up the poem he handed her and leaned back in a chair. A few moments after reading it, she slapped it down next to him and said, "Sounds like Robert Frost to me. Been reading *him* lately?"

"Well, no," Frank answered, visibly confused and hurt. He grew silent, muttering to himself, 'A writer needs fortitude; a little encouragement would be pleasant.'

He thought of Brid's being an ocean away and he had now heard from Don, who would be shipping out before the end of the month, most likely to boot camp in California, then directly to Nam. He now wished he had not shared his poem with Miho, who was now ignoring him totally and continuing to work over the light in the portrait. She was frustrated. She had not seemed impressed in the least with his effort at a poem. As nobly as he could, Frank reached for the poem, folded it, and put it away.

"What do you do on weekends, Frank?"

"Mostly I read, keep up with my courses, write, run, compete. What else is there to do in college? Get drunk? I don't do that a whole lot; actually— since I mentioned it— I've done it twice now. I'm counting. I don't want the number to get too high, higher than the digits on one hand. I don't like it much. I'd rather study."

"At two times, I'd say you're not in danger of ending up in AA. I have several friends in AA already. What do you have planned this weekend?"

"Nothing, just what I said, Miho. Why?"

"Do you have a car?"

"Yes."

"Well, would you like to take a drive up Steven's Pass? I'll even pay for the gas. I know some nice spots where we could camp. You could run up there on the trails, and relax. The snows about gone and there are probably some open areas for running. In fact, there wasn't much snow on the pass this year. It would do you good. Can you run at altitude that high?"

"Sure. It's good, actually. Do you think you know me well enough to go camping with me? You'd really want to go off in the woods with me? Even when you think I'm a plagiarist of Robert Frost's poetry? Besides, what's an islander like you going to do up in the Cascades besides long for your little grass shack?"

"Don't take the poem thing personally. I was toying with you. It's really a lovely poem. I'm frustrated with the portrait, that's all. You've got this jaw thing going on that I can't quite get the light right on. I'd just like to break away for a day or two from everything that I'm doing right now."

"I don't know that many women who would invite me off into the woods. Maybe I should be suspicious."

"Of what?"

"I don't know."

"Oh, yes you do. Go ahead, be suspicious! I don't think it's a secret. I like you. I'd like to see what it would be like with you all alone in the scary woods. I've always felt very free about things like that. I like you, okay? Does that make you nervous? Getting into the woods would do us both good. We might learn some things, don't you think?"

"I like you, too, of course."

"So what's to think about? Let's go. What happens *happens*, right? No need to trouble the water. We'll find a creek we can listen to and some animals to watch. My father used to tell me that running water will talk to you if you listen to it long enough. I think it might tell me what I need to know about you. Let's go find some running water and listen. We might learn a lot about one another. We might learn something we otherwise would miss."

"Like anything?"

"Like anything. So, now, what's with your jaw? I'm having trouble with the light on it. Did you have some big-boned ancestors?"

Frank thought for a minute and rubbed his jaw. "Actually, pictures on my mother's side of the family show some big-jawed Norwegians and Scots, now that you mention it."

"Hmm. I don't normally think of Northern Europeans in that light, but I'll look at some books in the library and see if I can get some ideas about how to handle the light at the upper end of your jaw and temple. Maybe it's just a random family thing and doesn't have to do with ancestors."

The next day Frank wrote the following dream fragment in his journal:

— *Miho said to me, "I like cities. That is, I like to go to cities. I like to go through cities."*

*

They had been driving for an hour. Miho was reading from *Le Petit Prince,* a book Frank couldn't decide if he liked. "To tame— to establish ties. . . . If I am tamed— we will need each other. . . . Please tame me— I have not much time, said the Prince. . . . If you want a friend, tame me. . . . You become responsible forever for what you have tamed."

Frank had a hard crush on Miho, but could not decide what message she was trying to send him.

"Do you like the book, Frank?"

"Oh, yes, well. It's an interesting book. I had a high school teacher who used to read passages from it. Frankly, I couldn't get my hands around it. I suppose it's meant as a guide to friendship, right?"

"Yes, I think so. And love, too, don't you think?"

"And love, too, sure, you could go that direction, too, okay," Frank agreed, watching the huge firs, hemlocks, and spruces race past the car windows. He passed a semi coming out of a curve as Miho leaned over the seat to get some sandwiches. Frank could smell her long perfumed hair. She smelled of chocolate, tea rose, and coconut.

"Love lasts," said Miho, "but friendships are tied to phases in our lives, don't you think? Don't you think that's the big difference between love and friendship?"

"I don't believe that altogether, but it does seem true to many friendships. Not many will weather time. You're probably right."

"I brought some coffee in a thermos; would you like some?"

"Yes, black, please, Miho, my-oh," said Frank.

"Like I've never heard that before," she responded.

Miho turned and got onto her knees in the seat to reach further into the backseat for the coffee. At the next curve her hip pushed into Frank's shoulder. It felt wonderful, but he resisted the feelings that were charging up like static electricity, unsure where they would lead. He was about to have a panic attack.

Miho was beautiful and Frank wanted a physical relationship with her, something that would last, but he could not seem to break the paralysis. He was driving and tried to keep his hands on the steering wheel. While he had never had complete sex with a woman, he had almost had intercourse with Brid several times. Neither of them had allowed the ultimate to happen when they were heavily petting. He missed Brid when he thought of making love.

"You know, Frank, this has nothing to do with St. Exupery, but you strike me as very unhappy in lots of ways. Don't you think the world is a fine place to be?"

"You, too, huh? Sure, I do. It's just the dark side of everything I can't forget. You have to work through things. I have an upbeat side. You can see that, I think. You wouldn't really want to be here with me if you couldn't see that. Other people look at me though and see me grappling with things. You become something from the things you grapple with and brood over. The Greeks used to say that character is fate. It's really as simple as that. If you don't work it through you don't grow your character. And the only good thing in that tautology is a tempered character. Fate without character is death."

"Oh," said Miho. "Like those fundamentalist road signs that say, 'the wages of sin is death'? The Adventists in Hawaii and the Philippines talk about that, too."

"Well, there's a possible connection, though St. Paul's aphorism was directed to Romans, as I recall, the believers of his faith in Rome."

"Frank, you don't have to let death ride alongside you in a car. You tend to carry your suffering on your sleeve. That's all I'm saying. At least Woody Allen can laugh at his moroseness."

Frank smiled. He liked her sense of humor and did not take it personally.

Miho looked at Frank as if he had something she needed. The signals snapped. He pulled off the side of the road and drove to the far end of a turnout, fighting his panic by driving along the gravel and listening to it pop against the tires of the car. Was he brave enough to handle a physical outcome with Miho? He was trying now, but trembling. The semi they had just passed crept up the highway and passed them as he flicked off the ignition key and put one arm around Miho. She was ready for touching.

It was happening finally, everything on automatic pilot. She stared in perfect stillness and curiosity, eyes reminding him of the liquid in an instrument. They made him move slowly at first, then he felt her kissing him hard and his arms were around her; she was pulling at him. Now her entire body was that fluid in the instrument. He closed his eyes and felt her being come around him like a giant surge of unstable water. He remembered swimming against the current in a storm, trying to make it to his sailboat before it drifted too far out of the shoals toward a deep channel. He recalled falling off a dock at the hot springs. He felt heavy and was going to the bottom of the spring. There were long murky green weeds flowing in the current and bits of broken algal blooms drifting past.

Within seconds they were fondling and taking each other's clothes off in the backseat of the car. He saw Miho's long black hair spread out like a giant sea anemone over his solar plexus and beneath her hair he felt as if he had just been hooked up to a milking machine. Sensual pleasure streamed from the outer nerves of his body right into his center. His panic was vaporizing and pleasure was overtaking him.

As Frank passively let Miho explore and press, he had enough sense to reach for his wallet. She was a sorority girl and he imagined that she would probably want to go all the way. He unfolded the wallet with one hand and slid out a cracked cellophane envelope holding a condom. It had been in his wallet for two or three years and Frank doubted whether it was good anymore. It had been folded so hard that it unrolled unevenly.

Miho watched him fiddling with the cellophane and started to giggle. He pulled her giggling wet face away from his body just in time and put on the condom. The demanding surge inside him stopped temporarily and he tried to be still. She was ready, but he realized he had no confidence in the rubber. She teased him, lying back, her hair wrapping across her shoulders and arms. She begged him with her eyes.

Frank did not say yes. He was too numbly throbbing with pleasure. He put his lips over Miho's wet mouth, then kissed her neck and tasted her puttylike nipples. As he closed his eyes he thought of Brid, whose nipples were like Miho's, but sweeter. Within seconds he slid his hand into the soft crease of her legs; they clamped him like smooth bark-stripped tree limbs. He pressed her into the ell of the backseat and after several dozen long and slow pumping motions through a small, scratchy entrance he felt her breath flutter. He tried to postpone the certain paroxysm of bliss that was overtaking him, but could not. He pulled away and released, immediately hearing another giggle displace Miho's erratic breaths. She was flushed and motionless now and he was hot and surprised. She was touching herself gently. Slowly they rolled to more comfortable positions and rested, feeling the warm sunshine come through the back window.

When he told her how long the condom had been in his wallet, she smiled.

"You'd like my father, Frank," she whispered effortlessly.

"Why?"

She was quiet for several minutes before responding slowly, "He talks about the dark side of life."

"I thought you were going to say something about condoms, that he recommends condoms."

"No," she laughed. "As long as there's pain anywhere in the world he's uneasy over his own pleasures. It's stoical, wouldn't you say? Well, that's my father. I can read it all over you now. You really regret what we've done. I could see it immediately."

"Your father sounds like a decent man."

"Look at that bear, she said, rising a little to look out the car window and pointing across the highway."

Frank looked and certainly there was a black bear walking along the side of the highway, an occasional sight along this stretch of road.

After putting their clothes back on, they drove up the highway to a turnout that Miho said would be there. As they drove along the rocky surface of the dirt road Frank could not keep from wondering about Miho's other sexual partners. He felt guilty because of Brid and was wishing he had given his virginity to her. What would he ever do with this new heaviness he felt about Brid? Now he had been unfaithful to her.

At the campsite they put up the tent and Miho joked that Frank had already used his condom; so now what would he do? He responded, "You are teasing me. I don't think we should have succumbed like that to our urges. It was bound to happen though, for me anyway. I feel like a member of the human race at last. I really like you, Miho."

"Frank. Stop talking. Virginal remorse is self-indulgent. Let's take a long walk along the creek. There's a trail over there." She pointed into the twilight.

"My eyes will take a while to adjust to this." Frank could barely see. The forest had become dark so quickly. He wasn't even going to challenge Miho's comment. She was worldly and she was right.

"Hold my hand. I'll be your guide," she said. Frank agreed and off they went. The air was cold. The creek whirred along the edge of a duff-covered embankment.

They spent an uneventful night in the tent and in the morning sat by the creek and had coffee and sandwiches. The sky pilot was blossoming next to low huckleberry brush. Miho put a foot in the water and exclaimed, "Liquid ice!" In speaking she startled two harlequin ducks that chased each other up the stream about fifty feet, then played tag splashing around a rock in the middle of the current.

Frank put his arm around her and she moved away slightly. He tried again and she reacted the same way. He said nothing.

"Look at the color in that water, Frank. See the violet and white when they splash together? I'm going to draw for a while."

"I'll grab your sketchbook and pencils," he said, dashing off to retrieve them for her.

"Thanks," she said when he brought them back. She gave him a kiss.

"Maybe I'll learn something by watching you. Before I do I'm going to walk up to that little falls." He pointed up the creek several hundred yards, then left her at the base of a cliff along the stream. As he walked he remembered the summer he and Don had worked for his uncle at the ranch near Bend, Oregon. They had fixed fence and watered stock. There was heavy timber and they cut firewood and ran logs through a small mill. The creeks were high when they began their work and low when they finished. It had been a beautiful summer.

After looking at the waterfall and the silty pools below it, Frank walked back and sat down next to Miho. She whispered, "Look, there's a fox."

Frank turned and saw the fox standing by a boulder near where he'd been walking. It watched them for a couple of minutes, then suddenly ran off into the firs and berry bushes. "Maybe I'll add that to the sketch," Miho said. "Don't you feel a part of this place, Frank?"

"Yes, I feel the mystery. There's a lot of power and strength and gentleness and stillness all around us."

"Have you ever been in love, Frank?"

Frank was surprised at the question, then thought to himself, 'What the hell. . . this woman is over my head. . . I don't think I could ever love her.' He said out loud, "Why do you ask?"

"A woman can tell if there's someone dear to a man she's making love to, especially if it's not her. I felt that in you. I like you, Frank. But I've never loved a man, really. I don't know what it will feel like because I'm sure it hasn't happened yet."

Brid was coming back into Frank's heart as Miho's spell wore off. He had never made love to Brid because he was always too terrified of getting her pregnant and not ready for the full responsibility of any accidents. He had somehow felt this would be the ultimate shame, not being able to follow through if he got her pregnant. He answered reluctantly. It would all just end badly for everyone.

"So *have you* ever been in love, Frank? Can you tell me?"

"Well," he said slowly. She was providing him with a context that he could step into, like an actor on a stage. Somehow he wasn't worried about her feelings for him or his for her. The openness was superb and unexpected.

"I have a close friend. I think I love her. We spent a lot of time together, especially in high school. I helped her. We helped one another. We were together mostly during the summers."

"Sounds passionate."

"Well, there's no need to be condescending. If you're in a rural community and you have a brain at all, you approach sex gingerly.

You don't just dive in the sack because you're hot for somebody. Chances are you'll have a little one to feed soon enough and that will switch your direction in life and everything will change, and you could instantly fall out of love if it's an accident."

"So you slammed on the brakes a lot."

"Listen. How'd you get to be so wise? *Of course, we slammed on the brakes*, and when I wanted to do it she couldn't say yes, and when she wanted me to I didn't have the courage. I never even thought about a condom until I was coming to the end of high school. Believe it or not, I thought they were a novelty item and not worth a dime. I didn't think they had any medical significance. I thought they were a joke to get people to have sex and make the manufacturer some money. Oh well. So much for hayseed ignorance."

"That's a convenient reciprocity for birth control: when you're ready, she's not; when she's ready, you're not. I wonder if Freud has an essay on that. At least you got some relief from rubbing each other."

"Oh, you really can bite, Miho. You surprise me with those little one-liners. How come you're so liberated?"

"Well, to tell the truth, I think it's because I knew nothing about baby-making at the time I felt my first really strong physical attraction to a boy. He took me swimming and got me out of my swimsuit and we were making out in shallow water. Before I knew what was happening he was inside of me, pushing me up in the air. I imagined a fish swimming up inside me. Then I broke inside. It hurt a little, but I was feeling so loose and warm for the boy that it didn't matter. I whimpered. He was sweet. Later on I didn't feel any love for him. He was a good person, just a very hungry one."

Frank was feeling vulnerable and transparent. He wondered if Miho would have him again. He didn't know if he wanted her. If she tempted him he would want her, but the way she was now was not sexual or sensual. She was talking like a guy in the dormitory.

"I was almost a virgin yesterday, Frank. I know what you are guessing, but I've only had three guys, including you. After the first one I had a boyfriend in high school. He was one of the smart ones. We had sex a couple of dozen times, usually with condoms. Once he pulled out early when we didn't have a condom, and nothing ever came of it. We drifted apart. I didn't love him. I don't think I've felt love yet."

Worried about his ego, Frank asked the standard needy question, "So what do you feel for me?"

"Frank, you're a terrific guy. You'd never fit in back home where I'm going after school. My family wouldn't accept you.

There's probably some family compatibility switch inside me that has to be flipped before I can really fall in love. I thought you might do it, but no. It's not going to be you, Frank. No offense.

"I do want to have at least one child someday. I'm afraid of marriage though. Our whole generation is. I think about pursuing a career mostly. I don't know if I can do anything in the art or design world, but I'm going to stay with it for a while and see."

Frank sat back against a stump and looked up at the green firs and cedars and gray snags all around them. The setting reminded him of his fishing trips with his grandfather Percy. Miho was grooming a small plant with her hand. Several crows landed opposite the stream bank. Time deserted them. A bluejay whipped over the water and disappeared into some trees. Every once in a while it would reappear, hopping higher and higher on limbs, as if using them as a ladder.

Frank was thinking about Brid. Did she love him? Had she loved him? He missed her and wanted to see her. Somehow he knew it wasn't going to happen. She would be different when she came back from Spain, as different as he was becoming.

She, in fact, had already been back in Lewiston from Spain for several weeks, but Frank had not yet seen her. She had given him the wrong return date and had come home earlier than he expected.

She did not call him immediately. There was a new uncertainty in her mind.

*

At Miho's party several weeks later Frank sat next to a man who was eating a huge brown cracker caked with goat cheese and slimy green hyphens. They reminded him of snail trails. He guessed that they had once been green peppers. Hearing the doorbell he answered it for Miho. A thirty-year-old man with a blond mustache and black leather jacket awaited a welcome. Someone yelled from behind him, "Miho, Tyler's here."

The person rushed up toward the door to shake Tyler's hand and welcomed him to the party. As he turned into the room Frank noticed the dark orange quarter moon stitched onto the back of his jacket, his long blond hair brushing the top of the moon.

Miho came up and said eagerly, "Frank, I'd like you to meet Tyler. Tyler, Frank."

"So, Frank, Miho has mentioned you. You were in an art class with her."

"Yes. She hasn't mentioned you to me. Are you in one of her classes?"

"Actually, I'm one of her instructors."

"What course?"

"Sculpture."

"Oh, the sculpture T.A.?"

"Yes, I'm the sculpture T.A. I gave up my associate's position in the philosophy department recently."

"Why?"

"I couldn't relate to the British mathematics fanaticism that is sweeping through the department. I also live on a farm up north of Monroe with my wife and two children. I live my day-to-day life in such a different world than academics do. I shovel horse manure, feed chickens, break water that's frozen in the drinking trough. It's a different world. I'm more interested in people and animals than ideas."

"I can relate to that."

Miho came up and kissed Tyler hard, then he put his arm around her. Frank got the message loud and clear and stepped back. Miho was happy and in most respects Frank was happy for her. He had known their relationship was going nowhere almost from the beginning. He had no resentment. She had not told him much about Tyler, but had certainly dropped enough hints to make him aware that someone special had stepped into her life. What she was going to do with a married man was an interesting idea, and he pondered it as he drank a glass of Chablis, then walked back to his dormitory room.

CHANGES AHEAD

After his short affair with Miho, Frank anticipated an avalanche of change. He wasn't sure he was ready for it. He would try to take it slowly.

Back from Spain, Brid was coming to see Frank, but he was no longer sure he wanted to see her. The affair with Miho had made him simultaneously ashamed to see Brid, yet eager to encourage her to follow her own dreams without him. The changes would come rapidly. He was now truly afraid of loving Brid, afraid that he would fail her, as he already had.

Brid got into Seattle late the night she came to see Frank, having caught a ride with a family friend. She was staying with a girlfriend from Lewiston who had transferred to the university. She was in a dormitory near Frank's and was to see him the next day.

"I'm glad I'm finally back," Brid said to Frank as she finally materialized and ran toward him. "I have looked forward to this day for so many months." She paused, then walked up to kiss him with her arms open, but he turned his head slightly to avoid the kiss. He squeezed her instead, then pulled away. Brid looked at his profile courageously, most of her words simply frightened out of her now. The message had been delivered. Frank had given her the first certainty she did not want. He turned to walk with her.

"Are we walking far?" she asked him.

"Not far. Have you heard of Buckminster Fuller? He's speaking tonight."

"Yes, I've heard of him, but have never heard him talk."

"He's very approachable. People call him Bucky. He's here, tonight, at the university. I've arranged for us to go hear him after we attend a party at the student center."

"I read one of his books, I remember. . . . Do you absolutely want to go to this party? I don't care if we don't do anything tonight. If you want to talk, I'd rather do that."

"They say he's a very simple man. It will be interesting. Yes, I'd like to go to the party and the talk. You'll enjoy going, I think."

"Frank, I really don't want to go. Why don't you go? I'll wait for you."

"I made the arrangements because you were coming. I did it for you. He's the kind of science person you'd enjoy meeting, very rational about method. We can skip the party."

"Thank you, Frank. I just want to be with you tonight. I only have another day here before I have to go back to Lewiston."

"Brid. I arranged this for you, for you to hear him. I don't understand. I'll be there with you. We can talk there and later. I'd like you to meet some of my friends who'll be there."

"Frank, you're pressuring me. I think you can tell we need to talk. Let's go somewhere quiet, away from everybody else, now. Anything but social gatherings tonight would suit me. I just want to be with you. Don't you see? You took me to a party last time I was over here, and a couple of lectures. Remember that party your bank robber friend from Los Angeles threw? Where do you meet these people? God! High life, low life. I can never tell what I'm in for with you these days. You know all the strangest people. Somehow they all like you."

"Brid, I want you to be happy. I think you'll really enjoy this lecture."

Brid was silent. She looked at Frank, then turned to walk down the hill. The sun was setting over the Olympic Mountains. Frank was angry, mostly at himself, but also at her. He clenched his fists and muttered, 'Just what I need right now, Brid walking off into the sunset.'

He followed her until she reached a park bench where she sat down. He sat, too. After a couple of minutes she pointed across a greensward to a small black rabbit sitting beneath a bush. The rabbit scurried around in some nettles, then ran off into the shrubs. A few moments later a rat poked its head out of some ivy, then disappeared.

"Okay, Brid. You win."

"I haven't won anything."

"I don't know how to begin. Things have changed. We've been good to each other for a long time. I now know that I'm the wrong person for you to share your life with. You might enjoy meeting other guys."

"There was just one thing I learned in Spain, Frank. I love you. Will you give me another chance?"

"What do you mean by saying, 'give me another chance'?"

"If you give me one more chance I promise I'll be good for you. I'll give you everything you need. I won't hold back."

"Brid, you're talking nonsense. You've always given me everything you could. I've never felt you haven't. I've never felt you hold back. And just because we've never 'done it' doesn't mean we blew it with one another. It's probably better that we haven't."

"I promise, Frank. I'll be better. I'll work harder. Give me that chance again."

"Chance has nothing to do with it."

"Yes, it does. After you left for school I confided in Don. I told him things I've never told you and he listened to me. He was kind. But more than listen; he seemed to understand me in a special way. We spent a couple of weeks together talking and walking. He even held me when I wanted him."

"He held you? Really? You're joking."

"Yes. He held me and listened to me. We didn't do anything more than that."

"Really?" Frank was stunned. "So my buddy was stealing kisses when I wasn't around. Why are you telling me this?"

"I thought you might know already. I thought Don might have told you and that was why you are so cold."

"No, he didn't say a word, but if I'd known I would have been cold. That's all you did? You didn't do anything more?"

"No, not really."

"What do you mean, not really? You did or you didn't."

"We almost did, but didn't. Anyway, it was just momentary. I pulled away from him, realizing I really wanted you and was just lonely for you. I was pretending you were him, in a way. I can't explain it, but it's over. The two of you seem so close. They say girls will do that, warm up to a guy who's close to the one they love. It never really happened with Don. Nothing happened. It didn't mean anything."

"You didn't make love?"

"No."

"You're not just saying this because it would be unbearable to tell me? or unbearable for me to hear?"

"If I loved Don at this point, now that would be unbearable to tell you. I don't. Let's just try again, Frank, with that behind us.

Odd things happen and people move on past. Everybody makes mistakes. We can't let them ruin us."

Adolescence had proved hard on both Brid and Frank. Many times they had almost made love, but at the moment of truth Brid would always say no; then, too inexperienced to imagine safe sex, Frank would find another solution to his age-old male frustration. Brid was too Catholic to go along with safe sex anyway, so her protective self-dialogue was always: Frank doesn't really want me; Frank would rather release himself than be inside of me.

Frank was silent. He was absorbing what Brid had told him. He felt betrayed, but knew that was unrealistic. After Miho he felt hypocritical. He had betrayed Brid. Any betrayal of his had now become pointless with Brid's revelation about Don. It was obviously over for her. It had never really been anything. It had not meant much more than exploration. She had possibly learned even less about herself than what he had learned about himself after having sex with Miho. This he couldn't tell Brid, not yet. He could hardly admit it to himself. He lived with his hypocrisy but did not pretend otherwise to Brid. In a way he was cold with Brid to punish himself for his behavior with Miho.

"Trying is not the answer," Frank finally said. "I think we use the word 'try' too freely. It's confusing. We should simply 'do' or 'not do' something because we know what our capabilities are. We should do what we have to do because we believe we can.

"So, can we do this again?" she asked sweetly.

"I don't think so, Brid. Not me. The fact that this is happening to us indicates there's something going on under the surface that's bigger than both of us. We've loved one another out of concern, wishing well, good will. We've helped one another. I think it's time to see that we're too different to continue. I've seen someone else, too. And it's not permanent, but it's made me realize there's something else out there for each of us."

"But isn't that why some people do continue? They do it because they learn they have a deep caring for one another? They 'are' different and they realize it? Frank, I don't care if there are a million options for me. I want you. I really do. I think you're not going to accept all of this overnight. It may take a while. Perhaps you have to find a way to forgive me, too."

Frank saw calmness in Brid, a strange steadiness. Perhaps she was breaking inside, but it didn't show. "Forgiveness has nothing to do with it. While you were warming up to Don I was warming up to someone else."

"Do you love that girl, whoever she is?"

"No," said Frank simply, ashamed that Brid appeared considerate enough not to ask for details. He didn't want to have to admit that he'd lost his virginity in a one-night-stand with a dried-up condom along the side of a dusty highway.

"Then I don't care about it. I want us to build our love from now, from what we know now. We have the future. It doesn't belong to anyone but us."

Her appeal affected Frank strongly, but he had lost a certain feeling for Brid and he didn't know how to retrieve it. He was silent again, trying to find direction in what was being said between them. He had deep, complex feelings for her, but was unsure what the changes they had gone through might signify about their future. Perhaps her fling with Don indicated a need for more experiments. He didn't want to be with her when she was going through them. He certainly wasn't feeling anything like the love she was talking about, especially after imagining Brid and Don in a half-clothed embrace. The idea of her with his friend had severed something inside of him and there was now a short in the wiring. The starter didn't work.

Brid was heavy-hearted and quiet. She visualized taking Frank's picture and putting it away forever. She couldn't think of a thing to say. The bushes and elms were all in shadows. A lamppost a hundred feet away popped on. "It's over," she mumbled. "It's all gone, ended, down the river."

Frank, too, was quiet. He didn't know what to do next. This wasn't easy. He wanted to say: "Let's get some sleep and talk about it tomorrow." Instead, he said, "I wish we'd both been coached better about what was ahead for us. We listen to the silliest things and believe them. We have all these noble ideas about what we can control in life. I'll walk you back to your room, Brid. I don't know what else to say tonight."

She wanted him to say: "Come stay with me tonight. We'll see how we feel in the morning." When she didn't hear this, she wanted to ask him to come stay with her, but she couldn't. The thought of it seemed too pathetic. Somehow she felt obligated to hold her desires in, to hide what remained of them. She was on her own now, and so was Frank. She was crying softly, which wrenched Frank's gut. He put his arm around her shoulders, but she was pretending it wasn't there. She would have to get by without his comfort, especially now.

Somehow she broke away from Frank and worked up the courage to say, "Frank, I'll walk back alone. Just come see me in the morning before I leave, okay?"

"Okay, Brid," he said, "I'll see you in the morning." He watched her get up and walk down the path. He said "good night" under his breath, but inside he was torn. He wanted a surge of love to boil up from deep inside his soul like a surging, boiling hot spring, something they could use as a source of goodness to save their relationship, but he was too cold where he needed to be at least lukewarm.

In the morning he showed up early at her room, but she was already gone. He had obtained what he did not clearly know he wanted.

*

The words of a song said something about bombers turning into butterflies. Another said the woman loved him up, and now he was down.

It had now been four months since that morning when he found Brid gone back to Lewiston. His relationship with her had been in his own brain now for that long. The only letter she had sent him over that time said she loved him more than ever and that everything was bound to work out. She wanted to see him.

Frank went to Lewiston but she would not meet him at her rooming house. Her new boyfriend dropped her off at the campus at Lewis & Clark. They met in the student center and had coffee. Brid wanted Frank, but didn't want him. She needed something else, a tether, a hold that was outside her relationship with Frank, something that would be there to comfort her when Frank was not with her or if Frank took her in, then turned her out again.

Frank felt like a lunatic. This strange love he had for this woman could not comprehend his abuse of her, but he was now snubbing her. In love, nothing will erode its last foundations faster. He could not see that she was reciprocating in her own way, anticipating his loss, reaching out for a hold on a different rock.

He imagined that if they separated for a while they could come back together stronger, surer of their love. They needed to loosen their ties so that they could see clearly what they truly wanted. Brid still loved Frank, he thought. She said so. He understood this intellectually, but emotionally he felt that what she professed was something she only wished she felt or could grasp.

The hardest moment for Frank, while he was trying to understand the law of 'appreciation through distance' was when he learned that Brid had become sexually involved with another man. He was not sure why she had told him of her new sexual relationship at a time when he was trying to sort everything out and determine if he could work Brid back into his view of the world, back into his heart to love her.

Meanwhile, she had made her assumptions. She was moving on despite all the hope he tried to build in himself. Here she was now sleeping with somebody else and still telling him she loved him. What did he need this for? He decided to write her one last letter:

Dear Brid,

I do not understand this love you profess to me. I got involved with someone, realized it wasn't the right thing, and got out of the relationship. I never stopped loving you, though it felt like I had for a short while. I'm coming around now and think of what we've shared over the years. I want it back so much. I do love you.

How can you love me, though, say you love me, and be with another man, sleep with another man and devote yourself to him? Are you nuts, or is this just normal? If it's normal in love, I didn't know it was. I must be crazy even to communicate with you about it.

Since our separation I have focused only on getting my career straightened out. I haven't dated anyone. I think only of getting back together with you some day by taking the right steps, whatever they are, however I can determine them.

Ever since winter there's been a shadow over this love and a harsh coolness. I get these letters from you, but do not see you much because you give me excuses. Our love is bread on water, increasingly irretrievable. I feel I have made every effort to adapt to you and this strangeness, but I now think of myself as a fool.

I love you, though our life together is over, apparently. I wish you the best, whatever the hell it means, and that comes from the depths of love and hope I still have. Does this make any sense?

I am trying to drown this candle.

Love,
Frank

Frank began recording in his journal a series of dreams about Brid:

— Brid drove by while I was helping a man into a detox center. She didn't stop. The man vomited everywhere. When I got him through the door of the center he said, "Thank you. Who was the dame?"

— Brid and her boyfriend skied past as I stood on a slope. The mountain was green and white and rugged. I felt the mountain wind on my neck.

— Brid and a new husband live in a little house with a smooth dining room table like the surface of a lake.

— Brid has two little boys with heads stuffed in milk bottles.

— Brid is with her child at the fair. The little girl walks up to me with a happy face. When I realize she doesn't look like me I turn away and the child goes back to its mother, puzzled.

*

In the fall, after a summer of work, Frank headed back to school, ready to take up studies yet again, uncertain of his future in the military. He had put off another talk with the commander for months, but knew his written request for exiting ROTC was being processed routinely. He decided to begin lobbying harder for release from the ROTC program. He also wrote several political letters to Congressional staffers in charge of military appropriations subcommittees. He thought it his duty to lobby against the war. The impact might be insignificant, he reasoned, but it would satisfy his conscience and maybe help steer the country into a more realistc course.

Meanwhile, Don had some time earlier been sent to Vietnam. Frank had only communicated with him once since he reported to a California boot camp.

Recently, the media learned that Nixon had secretly been bombing Cambodia. National Guardsmen at Kent State University killed four students and wounded eight others.

After going through the ROTC motions for five months Frank met the commander one afternoon on his way to the library. The commander paused, indicating he was going to speak to Frank. "By the way," the commander told him flippantly, not even looking him in the eyes. "You're out of the program! No penalties. Command informed me several months ago."

Frank was stunned. He said, "Thank you, Sir."

"No thanks to me, son. If I had my way you'd be digging privy holes in the jungles of South Vietnam." The commander turned and walked away contemptuously.

Frank was glad, but angry at the commander's manner and the fact that he had apparently withheld information from him deliberately. The military had made the decision about Frank a quarter of a year earlier, yet had given the commander free rein to harass or entice Frank for several months if he chose before giving him official notification of release. It was apparent that the commander was probably hoping that Frank would come by someday and tell him that he had made a big mistake and wanted to remain in the service. Frank would show up and say he wanted to stay in the military, in which case the commander would accept him back without contempt or spitefully kick him out of the program anyway.

Six weeks later Frank got a copy of his discharge letter. By then the posting date was over five months old.

SILENT NIGHT

The jungle was paisley green and white under the full moon. Phosphorus was everywhere in the trees, reminding him of snow.

Don lifted his rucksack and threw it over his shoulder. He ran for several hundred yards in the direction of his unit. The trail seemed different than the one he had come into the village on. He continued on, expecting it to become familiar, but he had come into the area during daylight, and there was darkness now except in the white powder falling from the trees. It fell around him like talc as he ran.

He continued up the trail another mile or two, but there was no sign of his platoon or other life. There was no more powder in the trees, only moonlight in the jungle. He still did not recognize the trail, but checked his compass and knew he had to be going roughly in the right direction. Perhaps the trail would intersect with the more familiar route.

Everything was dim as he gripped his weapon. The rifle felt as hard, heavy, and awkward as a rod of cut granite in his hand. An outline of hillside appeared off the trail to the right. To the left a paddy of the palest green opened up. At the far end of the paddy, near the jungle, stood a figure. Don stooped and lifted his rifle. The figure remained still. He slid the rucksack to the ground and dropped to a tripod position, bringing the figure into his rifle sights.

The moon slid behind a silky cloud, then reappeared. Reappearing, the moon seemed brighter. The figure now looked like a VC on patrol, but it was stationary, listening. Don expected movement, but Charlie did not move. Several bats broke the silence, darting across the paddy like swallows.

Don remembered going to the barn one winter night, in search of his father after he had not come in on time. His mother had grown worried. On the way to the corral Don saw a figure in the snow near the timber. It did not look like his father, so he stopped. It was a large animal on all fours. A quarter moon and several clouds played light over the trees and snow and as the moon cleared Don could see a crouching mountain lion. Still close to the house he returned for his rifle. When he came back outside, however, the animal had vanished.

Don then found his father cleaning the dairy cattle stalls in the barn, oblivious to the cougar's presence. He had not seen nor heard the lion. Stepping to the barn door they both heard the cougar scream in higher timber. That night they kept the herd in the barn, the standard operating procedure when a big cat was in the area.

The figure in the paddy was alone, though there seemed to be a cart or small building a few yards away. The smell in the air was of jacaranda and Don could not smell the usual gunpowder from his M-16. He watched for nearly a half hour and could still see no movement. The figure was steady, perhaps waiting for Don to make the first move. Perhaps it was a trap to pull him closer. Perhaps it was a member of his platoon, but he was not ready to take the risk of a callout.

Don began to crawl, inching his way across the paddy cautiously, keeping his trigger finger ready. The moon went behind a thicker cloud and remained hidden for several minutes as he crawled quietly, slowly.

Just as he was about fifty yards from the figure the moon came from behind the cloud. Moonlight shot along the edge of the paddy like a floodlight, coating everything with white reflection. Don was ready to call to the figure or command it, but just as the light hit he could see that it was a statue and the tiny building beyond it was a religious structure of some kind.

He walked cautiously toward the edge of the jungle, then alongside the figure: a life-size Kuan Yin with Vietnamese features. She looked at Don and smiled. Her message was clear: whether American or Asian, you will find silence, peace, and light where I am.

Don naturally knelt before the statue in the moonlight, stunned by the apparent message, one that had not needed to be spoken. He recalled a South Vietnamese soldier of Chinese background who had told him several stories about Kuan Yin. The one he remembered at this moment was that she, known as The Compassionate One, had once warned a warlord not to tell a lie to his guardian protector. "It will not lead to peace," she said, adding, "but he will find peace for you anyway and you will give nothing back."

The other story he remembered was less compassionate. Kuan Yin told a soldier carrying a torch that the torch would not only burn the tract of land he set ablaze. "It will turn on you and burn you in your own blood."

At that recollection Don got up and walked back to the trail, then headed up it in the dim light. He could now hear a jet behind him. Once on the ridge above he looked back toward one of the villages his platoon had ravaged. Another inferno of white phosphorus plumes rose from the jungle and paddies in the distance. The whiteness seemed to compete with the dark sky.

A CALL IN THE NIGHT

Dear Frank,

    I told you I'd write, so I guess I better. Everything is fine around here. Hank wanted to work here this summer, but we were afraid he'd cause too much damage. He was a good hand on the Ravan place for years, but he's always destroying stuff on ours. Vernon wants to find someone who can give him better help on the bottomland during hay season.

    I'm cooking elk stew and pies for dinner. No one ever gets enough elk minced-meat pie. Guess I better get back to it. You've probably heard the whole story on McNiese's nephew, Chuck, by now. He hung himself in a closet. Poor boy! We're all paying dearly for that war. I see a long line of soldiers in my dreams. They're going up and over a jungled hillside, like that old Yukon gold fields photograph at the library. I'm sure you've seen the one I'm thinking of. Be good.

Love,
SueLee

*

Dear Frank,

There's no reason to get upset yet, but Don's aunt called to say he's missing in action. She said the government told her that many MIAs show up sooner or later. Some of them go AWOL and I know you've said you weren't sure Don's heart was in the war. So don't jump to any conclusions yet.

I took your grandfather to the doctor. It seems that his shoulder is still bothering him, the bursitis. He sends his love.

Beullah sold two paintings last week for $70 apiece. The craft sales are way down though. She doesn't know if she can keep the business going.

Chuck McNiese killed himself. They found him hanging in a closet. He was that heroin addict who had to be rehabilitated. I don't think Ron McNiese wants anyone to know about the death, the same as he didn't want anyone to know about the drugs. You shouldn't tell anybody unless they need to know. There's no reason to gossip about someone who's had such a hard time. It's really really awful! Only God can deal with it.

I'll let you know about Don as soon as I get word. I'm sure everything will be all right. Don't worry.

Love,
Mother

*

The call came into the dormitory at two a.m. Frank was not sleeping well. "Hello?"

"Frank, it's Mother. We have heard about Don. It's very disappointing. This will be hard for you, I know."

Sitting on the seat in the narrow phone booth, half-awake, Frank felt the wave of terror clamp itself around him.

"They found Don. He was killed in action."

"God, no!" Frank said, stupified.

"He and two other Marines were killed by booby trap grenades. They got isolated near a hill after the rest of their group— a platoon, I think they call it— retreated from the area. They were lost and alone for several days before it happened. A routine patrol found him."

"God, no!" Frank's eyes erupted with tears and he felt completely helpless. He dropped to his knees.

"Yes, Frank. I know it's hard, Honey. We all know Don was a good person. He will be okay on the other side. He was the finest boy."

"How? But why Don?"

"These things happen, Frank. It's part of life. There's nothing we can do now. There has to be some reason for it. We'll all

understand someday. You will see him again. You know that.
We'll all see Russell and Sea someday, too. I'll go now and let you
try to find some comfort. Go ahead and cry. You'll feel much
better if you do. Just let the tears flow. I love you. There's nothing
more I can tell you now. I wish there were something else I could
do to make it easy for you, Honey. I'm sorry, Son."

"Goodbye Mother."

Frank left the phone and walked back to his room. When he got
inside he collapsed on the floor in the darkness. His roommate had
gone away for the weekend. He lay on his back, then on his face,
then on his back again. He imagined Don lying dead in the jungle
or in a box in the ground. 'This is what he will see,' Frank thought.
'Why Don? Why did it have to be Don?' he asked the darkness. He
sobbed and rubbed his eyes and could find no power to do
anything but lie still.

He fell asleep just before dawn and dreamed of his grandfather.
When the floor supervisor had first knocked on his door that night
and told him he had a call, Frank thought Percy had died. In his
dream Percy was lying half buried in the ground, upright like a
huge tamarack. His body was blowing away like sand in the wind.

*

Frank later learned that Don had been killed after the battle of Ho Summit, a battle that the U.S. military command set up as a publicity gimmick. A marine platoon was intentionally isolated; many soldiers were shot by enemy fire; then the commander in charge sent in helicopters full of newsmen to photograph the remaining soldiers fighting for their lives. There were many top journalism photo opportunities before several Phantoms flew in to level the jungle with napalm below the hill. One of the articles Frank read about the battle indicated that some soldiers may have been killed by friendly fire. Others disappeared after wandering off into the jungle and getting lost.

Frank missed the funeral two weeks after getting the news about Don, but he visited the cemetery near Upper Burnt Ruby Creek Notch on his next trip home. It was springtime, though winter had not released its grip on the wild mountain slopes and valleys of central Idaho. The road into the cemetery was still drifted closed, but recent tracks had left the drifts lower and they had melted considerably. He left his car at the gate and walked past a collapsing, weathered gray barn. He could see the sawmill below the O'Seetley ranch. Aspen trees gnarled by the snow were beginning to leaf out. There was smoke along the lower pastures from the bunkhouse of a nearby ranch's hired hand. The barbed wire fences were decorated with tufts of cattle hair and bent, dry timothy stems.

The wind on the mountain kept in Frank's face as he walked up the roadway to the graveyard. He counted the graves down from a trio of yellowpines growing at the top of the hill. There were spruces growing along the backside of the ridge and plastic flowers everywhere, wire stems wrapped around wreathes leaning against gravestones of granite and silica. There were crosses, books, and doorways made of pebbled concrete. A few new wooden plates marked some graves. These were routinely replaced every ten or fifteen years because they tended to rot away while lying atop the ground, decomposed by insect bores and mildew. Frank noticed several concrete buttons like hubcaps that had names written in simple cursive.

He read some of the names out loud. They were comforting: "Andrey May Hardin, Baby Boy Hardin, Sara Bell Barker, Alvin Blankenship. Frank Lacy McFall. Emma Lee Jasper, Charles A. Sult, Amos Buchanon, Orville Ket Apple, C.E. 'Ned' Blackstone, E.C. Broderick "Brod' Barker, Dollie Mae Ireland, Rufus Pierce, Russell Ravan, Sea Ravan, Warburg 'Deadeye' Pierce, Abraham Shira, Don Shira."

The snowy area around Don's grave had been dug away. There was an old ground squirrel burrow near the headstone. Don was the second Vietnam vet to be buried in the little cemetery that had only one WW I vet and one WW II vet. Frank smiled gently when he read Deadeye's real name. While Deadeye was alive, Percy had been the only one to know that Deadeye's first name was really Warburg. 'No wonder he had gone by the nickname of Deadeye all those years,' thought Frank.

He knelt on the ground and tried to be light-hearted. He put his hand over his forehead and wept, his chest contracting irregularly as he called Don's name, "Don! Don! My friend! My dear friend! I miss you." There was no reply as he invoked his friend's name. The wind continued blowing through yellowpine and spruce branches. A tumbleweed raced over the ground from a fence where melting snow had dislodged it. It raced down the hill and disappeared over a melting drift of snow.

DOWNSTREAM

Once apart, the end of the relationship came swiftly. Frank took up with a smart, wild girl from Coos Bay, Oregon, who seemed to understand him. Brid became more involved with wildlife biology and continued to see her new boyfriend who gave her the kind of constant attention and security she had always craved.

Frank last saw Brid on a visit to a Snake River birds of prey biology project. It was there, during a hike through greasewood, cheat grass, sage, and rabbit brush, he realized sadly that he and Brid had grown irretrievably apart. He resented the fact that she did not seem to know him well after all the summers they had spent together. From the things she said he pieced together the image she had of him, one she had no desire or ability to change. When he was around her he felt like he was in some kind of sealed box.

One of the last things she said to him as they watched dozens of Western tanagers flash over an eddy in the Snake River was, "I can't be serious all the time. You're no longer the happy person I used to love. You're so intense. It's hard to be around that. You talk so much about death. It makes me feel cold. I need to be light-hearted, free, warm, happy. I slowly realized, Frank, that I was feeling smothered by your stress. I still love you, but everything is mixed up now. . ."

Yes, thought Frank, Brid needed more attention, security, peace, a sense of upward mobility and permanence, direction, freedom, happiness. His world was too difficult, confusing, serious, intense, philosophical, even frightening. Vietnam was still raging and young men who were there or about to go there were lost about who they were. There was nothing simple and lighthearted about it.

Frank was wrong-headed about many things, but he swore to himself he was trying hard to change what he could and to know himself better. Shaking away his doubts about the war and the brooding it brought was still impossible.

"I can be lighthearted or easygoing," he told Brid, "but I can't be that way to hide something deeper that I'm feeling, so it doesn't trouble you. There's also consistency. I don't know where you're going anymore and your new relationships don't indicate a lot of love for me."

"It will be okay eventually," Brid said. "Give me time to find out more about who I am."

Great, an identity crisis, Frank thought. Identity crises are cousins of nervous breakdowns. Anything can happen from here. 'What are you wasting your time for?' he asked himself.

He traced his and Brid's difficulties to the time when his mind was trying to absorb new largely tragic events that did not square with how he expected the world to be. There were the deaths of Robert F. Kennedy and Martin Luther King, Columbia University's campus anti-war demonstrations, and Nixon's winning the Presidential election.

Frank was young, trying to do the right thing, with no experience. He was adrift intellectually, with no wise parents or sympathetic peers. American events from across the country seemed to pull him into the center of a thinking chaos, even though in reality he wasn't anywhere near that center. He sometimes felt that he was a captive of the mass media, but he could do nothing about it. College intellectual life dictated that national events should somehow guide the educational process. Even as he tried to pull himself away from the bigger picture of events and ideas they continued to dominate his thoughts. It was, he recognized, close to obsessive and a problem for anyone attending college during the 60s and early 70s.

For a while he was a premed major to try and adjust for a profession directed more to apparent community good, but he bailed out because it was too focused and routine and left all the big questions unanswered. He felt disappointed with his choice to try premed and also disappointed in himself for quitting.

To Brid this was immaturity at its worst, philosophy divorced from emotion and inevitability. Her uncle had been a WW II veteran and always talked clearly and confidently about service to his country in Italy and France. What could be simpler? she thought. Just do it, then come home to your girl no matter what happens to her in the meantime.

Before the very end Brid gave Frank a gift, but she had no idea she was giving him anything. Grateful for the blind offering— an introduction to prairie falcons— he later frequently recalled the cavity high in the rocks above the Snake River where Brid showed him several dozen pairs of young falcons squeezed together into recessed, thatched nests.

To Frank these wild birds symbolized all the courage, agility, hope, and clarity the world might give him. Their tiny eyes with the slanted, serious brows and pronged beaks gave him a new image for finding his way in life. He defined it as noble effort, purity of heart, and youthful awakening. He remembered conversations he'd had with Biscuit Laudon and the sense of freedom he felt afterwards.

As he walked along the canyon walls that day with Brid he also wondered at the northern harriers, ferruginous hawks, and hundreds of cliff swallows swarming near mud nests. Brid had shown these things to him and told him how the desert plants provided plenty of food such as ground squirrels for raptor prey. She explained how difficult it had been for the project to secure long tracts of brush as cover for the desert plants.

"All the farmers in the region want to turn the sagebrush into wheat," Brid said derisively. A wildlife volunteer with conviction, she knew all the history of the preservation effort.

During that long weekend as she spoke with Frank of their relationship, many of her expressions sounded recorded, as if she had been discussing what she was going to say to him after getting a coaching from someone she regarded as wise. Frank soon met the new wise one whose voice he had begun hearing in Brid.

The boyfriend had recognized quickly what Brid wanted and he tried to help her get it. From an early age she had longed to have the vacuum in her soul— left when her father died violently— filled with knowledge, accomplishment, security, and refinement. She wanted her father back or the best approximation of him she could find. Her mother had told her all her life what a fine man he was. In her student friend she found what she perceived as ambition, experience, and security, a reflection of what she desired.

Miho's seduction of Frank had been driven by curiosity, inspiration, passion, even idealism. The girl from the Philippines was worldly wise, sincere, and beautiful, while her successor from Coos Bay fed Frank's Promethean desires to break free, his intellect, love for equality, and openness. Janie was also quixotic and impulsive. Though she spoke like an amateur philosophy student, Frank didn't mind; he was searching and didn't care what his source of new ideas was. He was just thirsty for them all the time.

Brid had not enhanced any of these qualities in Frank, could not even see his need for them. She hated Frank's newest girlfriend, though she'd never met Janie and Frank had mentioned her only briefly. He had never discussed with the girl from Coos Bay his relationship with Brid. To Brid, Frank's new companion represented mere fantasy and oblivion. Brid wanted her cake and to eat it, too. She wanted Frank but didn't want him. She knew very little about Miho, on the other hand, and didn't care because Miho was no longer with Frank.

Meanwhile, Frank hated Brid's boyfriend Max who had robbed Brid of what he felt was genuinely honorable. He felt Brid was no longer honest about anything, though she talked about honesty more than ever.

Her seduction had taken a different form than Frank's. Her companion was openly vain and, after being introduced, told Frank scornfully one afternoon, "Brid told me all about your problems. She's had difficulty over deciding whether she wants to help you with any of them."

This astonished Frank and ignited his hatred, but he endeavored to be civil, to show Brid that he truly cared about her desires, and respected her choices and needs, no matter what the results might mean. He could not dispel the sense that manipulation was fast becoming the force of the day. And he refused to play games with Brid when she quietly whimpered that she wished Frank would just spirit her away from all the new directions in which she was headed and the new inclinations she was having.

Frank tried to make sense of the end of the relationship. He had for too long been afraid of getting Brid pregnant. It had become a terrible fixation offset with the weaker drive to achieve something more important: education and training so they could build a family together. Obsessing on satisfying his woman sexually, the dangers of penetration, and the psychological interference of his crazy religious mother and the monkeys on her back became the main distractions in Frank's mind. It was a torment that it took him many years to understand.

Maybe Frank had failed to hold fastidiously to good humor at a time when young men faced terrible decisions of conscience over Vietnam. He was too self-reliant and had proudly acquiesced to a new social diversity beyond Anglo-Saxon mores, social ideas that embraced as equals Semites, Africans, Hispanics, and a newly revealed behavioral entity: homosexuals. It was hard to put it all together into a new, acceptable framework. And he could not talk with Brid about any of it. She had always looked at him with such disdain whenever he tried to talk about the revolutionary social changes that were sweeping the country and the regenerative attitudes of interracial and sexual cooperation and toleration.

Somehow he knew that his brother Sea had been a young, probably not fully aware homosexual. This knowledge had melted Frank's fear and distrust of gays. When he learned of Sea's inclinations, homosexuals instantly became human in his mind and with all the personal rights of anyone else. Frank had found a book in some of Sea's things after he had died and he had taken it to a college professor to discuss. The book, called **Boise Boys**, was a stunning revelation to Frank that he accepted reluctantly at first, then readily. He learned that the book was a cult classic that told of a thriving gay underground in a Western city on the edge of the Great Basin. Frank kept the book away from his mother and Percy, realizing that its contents would be unacceptable to them. He also was the only one who knew that the book had probably been given to his brother by Dirk Lucas, a young man he had always thought his brother disliked. Dirk's name was on the inside of the book's cover.

Frank prided himself on his respect for Brid and never discussed their relationship with anyone else. To him this would have been infidelity. In this pure way, he remained faithful to her in his thoughts, respectful of her, hoping that somehow they might come back together.

Leaving Brid to her wishes, projections, and desires, however, became much easier for Frank after conversing with her arrogant, yearning lover. Frank now saw her contorted thoughts and emotions reflecting someone he did not respect.

Someday Frank knew that he would be able to leave his own self-righteousness about the relationship behind and walk away without contempt for anyone, including himself. He knew he had not been a perfect companion for Brid, that he had neglected her in many ways.

Still, for a long while after he stopped seeing her, she continued to write him earnest, emotion-filled letters that seemed like she thought Frank was the end of the world, the light of her life. She spoke to him of her love and the beauty of being in love with him, about how it was so sad and impossible to think of him with any other women.

*

254

Dear Frank,

I still miss you so much and wonder all the time how everything could go as wrong as it has. I am back at school and taking some new science classes. I can do all the work I need to do, but I am always thinking of you.

Couldn't we get together for a few days when the term ends and completely start over? I would love that more than anything else in the world. You are the only one I have ever loved and I hope we can find a way to start again. I am sometimes torn between thinking I'm being sentimental over loving you and really loving you.

I have regrets. Maybe I have lied in the past, but I want something better. I could be good for you.

Love,
Brid

*

At the time that she wrote him these letters, she was still with her newest pal Max, whom she had undoubtedly only left momentarily so that she could pen a letter to Frank. As Frank realized this, again and again, her letters carried less and less meaning. The expressions of her love seemed increasingly to be beautiful missiles falling short of a target. He spent long hours wondering how a woman could tell him that she loved him and him alone, then turn around and bed another man and share his deepest intimacies. The loneliness must be profound, beyond anything he wanted to experience himself.

Frank was obviously growing up, but it was still a long time before he perceived Brid's loneliness and fear as pathological. He occasionally conjectured that her behavior might be so common as to make all relationships frightening, terrible things.

Still he found himself sometimes believing in her ever more faint cries of sincerity, her longings, and love-filled letters, her promises to turn back into his life and make something they could both build into a future. It was difficult not to believe her siren song even after he had trapped her in dozens of pathetic lies. She even wrote once that Frank probably saw her as a "compulsive liar," then she added, "well, perhaps I am."

Love originating in puberty had supported all the best and worst in human needs. It had fed on them for health and illness. It was time to move on.

Even after Brid said goodbye to Frank one final time, she still continued to write him the same abiding letters of love. Frank began to have a recurring dream. In it he was a teenager:

— The setting is usually a carnival where I hold the hand of a little girl of six or seven named Brid. She is trying to find her father, and during the dream as she searches she grows into a young woman.

In the last of these dreams he had desired Brid, wanted her attention, love, and warmth; yet he expected her to be distant and unresponsive. He was surprised when she wasn't:

— She is at the carnival, loving, warm, happy, respectful, loyal. She is my age and holds my arm as we walk about the fairgrounds. She won't leave my side until we come to a man who looks like her uncle, Old O'Seetley, who is splashing around in a huge pool of water. There are trout everywhere and O'Seetley is catching them with a net, fat trout with large intelligent heads and green speckled backs. As he catches the fish he mounts them on plaques and hangs them on a wall by the pool. Brid leaves my side and walks over to the wall where she kneels down and prays to the shrine of mounted fish.

Frank had thought enough about his own dreams to know that the trout represented his desire for procreation. He also knew that procreation with Brid— no matter how sexually satisfied he might become— would be controlled solely by her paternal images, needs, desires, and a deep void from wanting something she could never have. In her ongoing loneliness she would always find ways to betray him and the others to whom she clung and she would get better and better at hiding these betrayals. Frank did not know who or what was the true essence of this woman, whom he had loved for so long. He barely understood himself.

When he comforted himself with Percy's last remarks about Brid, he tried to delete the smug feeling behind them. Percy had said, "Just remember that she was O'Seetley's niece. If you just went to our water company meetings you wouldn't have known that O'Seetley was a liar and a water thief. A commissioner who had never been to one of our meetings before, said to me after one that O'Seetley impressed him as a very honest man. I told him that he should come to my spread in late August and that I would take him out to the 160 above the Jameson place. I did take him out there in August and he took several pictures of diversion dams that only O'Seetley could have or would have placed. At the next water meeting O'Seetley said he was being framed and that while he may have 'snitched a little water' in the past he would never do it now."

*

Frank walked out of the heaviest rain and into the logging camp bunkhouse where water spilled through the cracks of shabby tamarack shakes. There were puddles of different sizes scattered from the kitchen doorway to the far wall of the long bunkhouse. Bunks untidy with green canvas sleeping bags and dirty clothes hid dust bunnies and shanks of smoky bronze beer bottles. He walked to the window, away from the room's stale odor, and heard a voice outside, "Pull that truck into the shop and we'll put new bolts in the tie rods."

From the window Frank saw the foreman in a green flannel shirt, black stocking cap, and logging boots, walking toward a line of trucks. As the rain drenched him, he walked stooped like a hunchback. Soon a diesel engine growled and a logging truck rolled mightily into the hangar-sized shed, bright red brake lights flashing against the shed's wet door jambs.

Frank buttoned his jacket and slipped out the back door again, then down a narrow trail lined by gnarled roots, willows, mountain ash, and yarrow. The rain continued torrentially, but did not penetrate his heavy wool mackinaw. Reaching the river, two ruffed grouse discharged from a bank of sagebrush and whistled into a gully full of scrub alder and cobblestones.

At the middle of a metal and tamarack-beamed bridge he leaned against the railing. Beyond the corral along the river he saw the cabins and bunkhouse of the logging camp and on the other bank a slender aspen, branches flying with each gust of wet wind. Green leaves danced circularly in mottled sunlight; the cloud cover was breaking up.

In the deformities of the limbs Frank saw a woman, her body cold and moist, ugly and lifeless. With more light the form freed itself, grew beautiful, and danced, lifting hands to breasts, face, and eyes. When the temptress was about to speak, the aspen whirled her away without words, and clouds in the shape of giant wings closed over the sun. Carved into the walls of a thunderhead, Frank imagined another faint image, then he shook it off and chastised himself for daydreaming.

He looked down into the mountain water as a chainsaw started up the canyon. Its pitch waved steadily until the sudden silence announced a coming vibration to the bridge's beam works. The tree hit the ground as Frank reached into his chest pocket and took out a grainy photograph, then dropped it into the river and watched it turn clockwise in the current. It grew smaller as it drifted away. The artifact would provide momentary interest for a steelhead fisherman downstream. The image would soon fade: the fine, black bangs, worn leather coat, deep dimples, prominent nose, and wide blue ribbon in the hair. Brid's eyes said one thing: "I have what I think I need. Goodbye."

GATHER AT THE RIVER

Bern, impatient for the snow to withdraw, had decided to test
the waters of Upper Burnt Ruby Creek early that spring.
Crawford's Nook was not thought of as a river community. The
river was not the center of life the way it can be in a river town
where a good part of the economy is tied to what happens on the
river. Lewiston is such a town in Idaho where the force of the
Clearwater and Snake join and eventually add to the Columbia as it
flows to the coast. Payette is also such a town, where the Payette
River joins the Snake on its way to pick up waters from the

Salmon River that works its way across the mountains of central Idaho.

Crawford's Nook derives its identity from its history as a high valley trainstop surrounded by mountains and streams. The Upper Burnt Ruby Creek is only six to fifteen feet deep in the spring and two to five feet deep in the summer, but its waters in April and May are charged with power matching any other similar moving body of water in the territory. A handful of other nearby creeks are as strong, but none of them singly dominate the character of rural life, except perhaps the South Fork of the Elk Fork River. Sometimes Bern chose that body of water over Burnt Ruby, but not this year.

Upper Burnt Ruby waters begin merging at eight thousand feet and by the time they reach a mile high they have gathered all the waterpower of a thousand small springs and rivulets. In spring this power is unmatched, with heavy waters plunging tightly between shorelines only fifteen feet across in some places.

Bern always respected this power by traveling with the force, never defying it. When she slid into the icy waters in the spring it was always to accommodate the deep and rapid creek. She had no desire to do anything but ride with its playful currents for several miles below the notch, then to exit slowly along a long sandy bar near Jorgy's ranch, to slowly roll up against the sandy embankments and pull herself up to a fire that she would build there. She always stashed clothes and kindling at her exit spot before going upriver to dive in.

She could tolerate the cold water because for her it was like coming to life. The shock of the spring runoff against her body that had for long wintry months avoided cold was a way to start anew. She had always dared her brothers to swim with her in the spring, but they always eschewed her suggestion. She swam alone every spring for an hour or two, always happy to be a child of the creek and disconnected from everything for just a while, flashing along in the water like a wood duck, sometimes submerging, then reemerging with a wild shriek.

Today was no different than any of the other days of spring when she had pulled herself from the routines of the ranch and gone off to the high shore just below the Notch. The sky was gray and the light muted to a hazy orange. Clouds kept knocking out the light momentarily, then it flooded back and illuminated the shoreline of the creek, its tamarack and lodgepole thickets butting against huge boulders along the shore. She slipped off all her clothes but a light blue one-piece bathing suit and stepped past an old log that had rolled halfway into the water. As her legs brushed past the log she felt the water begging rudely to pull her under the deadfall and a long submerged curtain of still green branches. Usually when she felt this force she knew it was time to go with it, to let the water have its way. She would feel abandoned for only a few seconds, then the power of the water would have her and yet protect her. As long as she gave in she knew she would have no problems and that the currents would play with her, toss her about, tease her with not letting go, then they would suddenly release her and let her body float to the surface and gambol on down the rapids, tugging and pushing at her lightly as she went.

Standing in the water up to her thighs the river began its prodding, then as she slid down further up to her neck the river took her with the force of an avalanche. She could delay no longer but was now churning in a tube of torrential water pressure under the old tree with the many limbs. It seemed stronger than ever, like the weight of a truck pushing on her, making her go harder and faster than she ever had. It was not easing up as she gave into it; it was bearing down on her, its weight of tons of water forcing her before it, not playfully this time, but demandingly. Her sense of being centered and able to participate in what was going on around her seemed different than usual. This was violent force bearing no intuitive promises of protection. It was dominating and fearful, and it would not let up even for a second. It kept bearing down on her until she felt the pressure was making her exhale. This was the beginning of her terror. The knob of a broken branch plowed into her thigh as she was sucked into it and immediately past it. Now she would not have any breath in her lungs to protect her until she could get another breath. There was too much weight on her. With no oxygen she felt forced to breathe the water. She held off as long as she could but her head was starting to burst. She needed to breathe in. She had to. She silently begged the water to let her have a breath, but today the water paid her no attention. It just drove her down along the bottom of the creek and began rolling her like a rolling pin on the bottom of the stream. She felt the pain in her thigh and knew the river was now taking her blood. She was not giving the river anything today but it was taking what it wanted.

Her bruised and punctured body was found two miles downstream from where she had planned to exit. Jorgy and Sheriff Altman, Fitz's replacement from Challis, Idaho, found her, tangled in the muddy root system of an upturned yellowpine along the shore. Her swimsuit was gone and the body had been rolled in so much sand and mud that Jorgy told people later she looked like a pig in a blanket. He stuck with that description because he felt it more dignified than saying her naked body was wedged in the roots of a pine tree where he had to cut her red hair loose with a bowie knife.

When Frank learned of her death he could not believe it. It was unimaginable that such a happy creature would end her days in such a tragic way. He begged SueLee to tell him it was not true, but she just looked at Frank and said, "It's truer than true, Frankie. Truer than true." By her raw red, sandpapered cheeks and unlubricating tears he finally got the message, but he did not readily accept it. He had to go back and review every death he knew about so that he could somehow fit Bernice's passing into its rightful order in the list. There had been so much accidental death. It always came unexpectedly, too. He could never see it coming. It always made him jittery afterwards for weeks, because no planning could prepare one for the surprise of learning about a disastrous demise.

The forces of nature have no friends in the human race. They are at odds. Yet humans continue to skew the line of separation, not realizing when they have stepped too far off track. Then it hits with power; the deed is done. It's over and everyone has to pick up the pieces and try to make some sense of it. This time Frank did not know if he could do it, just file it away, classify it, just portray Bern as an innocent victim of forces she did not understand or fear.

It was hard to do, but Frank knew for his sanity he had to have a mission statement associated with Bern's death. It was expected of one.

The problem of evil here, Frank thought, is that even innocents can make mistakes, and the size of the mistake is equal to the size of its repercussion. No one is protected from some accidents. Had Bern been more thoughtful or knowledgeable that day the water might not have taken her. But she was only thinking of the best of her experiences and had no fear of something that had always been good to her.

WIND

The wind was so strong it was shaking the house. A skiff of snow blew crystals off the ground and into eddies below the cabin eaves. Frank sat in the chair in the alcove, the window open, the creek trickling in the background. He could see the big white frame of Matthews Ridge between gusts.

He remembered walking with Don along Weldler's Lake in the spring, listening to loud cracks like distant thunder as the lake thawed and split. They often talked of the storm that caught them off the peninsula and turned their sailboat upside down, breaking their mast. They were close enough to shore to swim in, pulling the sailboat slowly with them, fighting the current. They had talked that day of the last time either of them had seen Badger Pete, a miner Frank's father Russell had unearthed from a snowy grave one spring. He had died of exposure after a long trip through the snow to obtain supplies.

Frank knew the mountain spirits of coldness, beauty, forlornness. Growing up on Upper Burnt Ruby Creek he knew them well and they caused a deep ache in anyone who spent much time in the high country. One could feel the wind, touch the trees, hike the steep beautiful slopes, hear the screaming rainstorms tear at the faces of lakes and mountainsides. The feeling took over one's soul.

Frank got up and went outside in the wind where an aspen trunk was nudging the side of the roof. The moon had risen in the west, a misty white crescent over a now black mountain. White and gold stars appeared from behind gunmetal clouds that swept along the slopes. Red sparks from the chimney blew over the roof and onto the balcony and several landed on Frank's neck and burned him gently. He shook them off and felt the spirits of the dead in the wind, those who had lived in the mountains and died there. They seemed to travel in the beautiful wind at night, after they had died, reluctant to leave any of it behind, reluctant to go on to greater beauty, higher places, or other kinds of existence outside the cycles of earth and water and wind.

Before going to bed Frank wrote a strange poem to his dead brother Sea, commemorating their love for lonely alpine beauty:

Loneliness my brother
I walk with you
Never lost in you
I give you all I have
Care for all we share
All that you encompass

If necessity brings poverty
I thank necessity
I see too much
Understand too little
The wisdom of this
High country forlornness

Shaken, frail, ruined
Those who do not know
The unfailing calling
The strength in detachment
Deep, lovely, gentle
Close around one

The peace in
Seeking until cold

Service forever
Teaching the oneness
Kindness of this place
Like wind it never fails

*

In his journal under the category 'beauty' Frank included the following entries:

— *At the first snow I was hunting. I got caught in a one-room cabin on the South Fork breaks of the Elk Fork River. Fortunately, there was a gas stove and plenty of propane. I got very warm before hiking out eight miles in two-foot deep snow.*
— *There's a coyote in the sagebrush and some yellow flowers. The first calves and lambs of the year are out on the slopes. Red anthills are being built after having been leveled by the snow.*
— *The annual porcupine race in Fell Creek is inhumane. Porcupines are caught in garbage cans and released onto a football field where the first one to cross the finish line wins a prize for its captor: ten cases of beer. The captors encourage the porcupines to the finish line by standing behind them and whacking garbage can lids with mallets. The noise maddens the animals and they rush forward.*
— *There was a dead bird in the shed: feathers everywhere. I spent the rest of the day driving Sloan's Point Lookout road. There was heavy smoke in the valley and treetops along Lake Fork Creek. I also saw two ghosts standing by the woodpile at the Sanford cabin, drank coffee, fixed the snow cat, fed the horses, got out of the late afternoon rain, argued with my Indian crew, listened to squirrels, replaced several radio antennae. A deck of logs rolled into Kennelley Creek. I took a cold bath trying to set a choker. Redpolls made a racket. I saw an eagle and one mule deer. I*

caught a glimpse of a deer standing at the salt lick in the moonlight. Afterwards I took a walk in the field in the rainy darkness. There I frightened the mules that were certain I was an evil spirit or a mountain lion come to dine on them.

— The rain falls steadily into the pastures. I watch from the cabin window. The black pines along the river hold the mist. The table is full of letters, reviews, books, tobacco tins, matches. When I let the fire go out, the cabin gets cold quickly.

— The bunkhouse has some loose shakes I need to fix before the entire crew moves in. The mattresses need a good airing in sunshine.

— I was alone yesterday in the large meadow, working the snow-beaten fence line. Spring winds were blowing hard off Matthews Ridge, thawing the snows anchoring the wastes of lodgepole, fir, tamarack, and yellowpine. The snowcat was broken down again, so I was working from snowshoes. The horses and mules will be here in a week or two. I'll be kicking apart big yellow hay bales for the animals soon in pastures still icy in the mornings. The bivouac is still in good enough shape for another season. It's old, but the pillars are made of twelve-inch yellowpine.

— The fields will soon be full of dandelions, bluebell, mustard, and fireweed. There'll be wildcats and cougars to contend with for several months, especially after the sheep come into the upper valley.

— I broke the wirestretchers and had to walk back to the shop to fix them. Upper Camp Creek is swollen where it joins the Upper Burnt Ruby Creek. Taking the shortcut back I had to wade it and nearly froze to death.

— At sunset the other night there was a double glow. After the radiance had subsided and a bank of gray clouds darkened the valley, a second sunset opened to the west like a huge orange scar. A lightning storm began over the valley. I noticed a deer near the barn watching me closely and sensed its fear, but it stood its ground motionless even when the thunder burbled in the distance. Suddenly the wind slammed one of the barn doors shut and the

sound was louder than a rifle shot. The deer leapt straight into the air and was gone immediately. I laughed.

— Snow's coming off the roof. In the morning when it is still cold, some of the ice that falls breaks into glassy dust. It blows up against the cabin. Chunks of snow blow off in the wind like broken angel wings.

— I remember stories Biscuit used to tell me about soaring around the sky at night. Perhaps this was one of those experiences. It wasn't a dream. It was real. The hike down to the lake took about an hour. After dinner at the campfire I hiked out a grassy peninsula into the center of the lake. There I unrolled my sleeping bag. It is summertime, ten p.m., and the stars are out. Opposite the gray-brown mountain sculpted by back-lit shadows the sky is a huge blue dome dotted with a billion starlights. As I lie down on the narrow peninsula and look up and around me I can see only heaven. Looking to my right and left I see dark mirrors speckled with light. I am relaxed, feeling everything. The water is black and the speckles are in perfect symmetry. I am almost asleep but float upward into the surrounding air. I feel closer to the stars than ever. There is a violet ball of light high above, maybe several miles up. I glance to my right and left and the dark mountains are interlocking crescents below, spreading east and west all the way to the Montana and Oregon borders. The horizon is arched and the mountain I camped below is far beneath me now. I see it when I sit up and look around. I lie back down and look at a ball of violet light that is spinning slowly and glowing faintly. I feel peaceful and fall asleep. I hear water lapping the grass at the drop-off shoreline; it is speaking to me in a language I would like to understand; I am learning what I can.

SEA'S DREAM

Frank remembered a dream Sea had described to him a week or two before he died. It gave Frank comfort remembering it; he was not certain why. Perhaps because Sea had described most everything in the dream as exceptionally beautiful, and what wasn't beautiful was still somehow acceptable in some bigger context that was not entirely understandable to human beings.

From an elective college course in art Frank remembered an Austrian artist by the name of Cranach, who painted large murals of elaborate hunt scenes with nobles and their weapons on horseback hunting wild antlered deer swimming deep water, distant castles, and nearby pastoral dramas of tethered hunt dogs and dead game. When he observed some Cranachs in an art history book he immediately related them to Sea's dream.

In Sea's dream the landscape was dark green with pine, spruce, and tamarack trees. The shape of the mountain in the background was like Bird Ridge, very steep on one side. Down in the depths of the timbered slopes one could see Deadeye's mine entrance and Deadeye standing next to his mining train cars. In the foreground was the lake where Frankie and Sea had first watched loons dancing in pre-dawn light, and Jimmy Samsin was standing along the shoreline. At the center of the mural were Russell on his giant Morgan horse named Flint and Biscuit Laudon on his Appaloosa. They were gazing at a field full of deer drinking near the old spring. A pile of dirt shaped like a horse was at the edge of the field, with huge butter-colored and black daffodils growing on top of the mound. Both Frankie and Sea thought instantly of the horse old Aatta Hourula had murdered.

In the woods near the lake one could also see a bookcase full of records, like the one Sea had kept in his room for years. Overhead in the sky above Bird Ridge was Russell's friend Martin waving from the cockpit of his Bucker that was flying into the sunset. To the left of the mountain in the clouds were two angels' faces and little white wings whipping the air like a humming bird's. Closely looking at the faces Sea said he could tell one was Solonge Naul, whose brother had accidentally killed her in a hayloft, and Joleen Olbaleen, whose husband had beaten her to death.

The whole scene was bucolic on the whole, and Frank always remembered the joy Sea had when he was telling him about it. It gave him no sadness to see representations of those who had died. The vision the dream inspired only flooded him with joy, he said, because the mural as a whole was so beautiful. He said it seemed that everything would be okay, that everything in the scene had its place in a bigger picture that seemed unclear.

Frank knew he would never completely know the reasons for all the good and bad he experienced in life, but he accepted what Sea had said and tried to extract some meaning from it, not really philosophy.

He agreed with Sea when they talked about God and religion. Sea said that real religious belief could never reflect ultimately the reasons for our being, but only hint at ways we could adapt to the mystery, accept the mystery. This was enough for Frank most of the time when he lay troubled over death or loss. He frequently remembered the dream of the mural and the things he and his brother had discussed. He sometimes added to the mural in his own mind as he fell to sleep at night. Standing near Jimmy Samsin he could see Tom Petrella and Billy Naul, and another angelic face shone near Solonge and Joleen: Bern. But primarily he remembered his encounter with the lynx on a cold winter night. He sometimes placed the lynx in a patch of snowy woods on the edge of the dream canvas. In the background he visualized the hull of the bulldozer. He also added Percy sitting in his chair by a swollen Upper Burnt Ruby Creek. Together these images helped him complete his recollection of things that made him desire wisdom.

The End

Acknowledgments

I wish to thank Mike DelGaudio of Creative Commons for the cover photo: straight outta the camera.